The Doctor Meets the Boogeyman

The Doctor Meets the Boogeyman

Matthew Petchinsky

The Doctor Meets the Boogeyman
By: Matthew Petchinsky

Disclaimer:
This is a fan-made work inspired by the *Doctor Who* universe. It is not affiliated with, endorsed by, or connected to the BBC or any official *Doctor Who* license holders. All characters, settings, and concepts from *Doctor Who* are used in a transformative, non-commercial, and creative manner under fair use. This book is intended purely for entertainment—created by fans, for fans.

Prologue: The Nightmare Begins

The inky expanse of space rippled with whispers. Shadows twisted and coiled through the fabric of the cosmos, unseen by mortal eyes yet felt deep within the soul. The Doctor, often celebrated as a hero, a healer, and sometimes a savior, had faced monsters, madmen, and the unthinkable terrors that dwelled at the edge of reality. But this—this was different.

The nightmares had been relentless for weeks. Sleep, that rare indulgence, had turned into a realm of suffocating darkness, where time itself seemed to stutter and fray. In these nightmares, the Doctor found themself standing in a realm that defied reason. No stars shone there; instead, the abyss gaped wide, pregnant with an ancient hunger. An intangible pressure filled the air, pulsating with a presence that whispered of unfathomable age and malevolence.

Each night, the Doctor's subconscious was ensnared deeper. Tendrils of thought reached out like skeletal fingers, whispering words in a language older than light, promising secrets that were never meant to be known. The dark corners of the universe hid many things, but this presence—this shadow—was unlike any the Doctor had encountered. It was an entity without a name, for to name it would grant it form and power. Yet, in the pit of the Doctor's dual hearts, it was known simply as *the Boogeyman*.

Far away, in a modest, timeworn house nestled on the outskirts of a quiet English town, a child named Emily lay curled up in her bed. Moonlight filtered through the curtains, casting pale streaks across the room. Her eyes were wide open, reflecting that silvery glow as she stared at the door of her closet. It stood ajar, a sliver of darkness so deep it felt like a gateway to another world. The silence of the room was punctuated by the creaking of floorboards, the house's groaning breath, and Emily's own quickening heartbeat.

Her parents had long since dismissed her cries. "There's nothing in the closet, Emily," her mother had said, smiling wearily. "You're safe, sweetheart." But Emily knew better. Something had been watching her. She could feel its gaze, cold and relentless, waiting for the moment when the darkness would thicken and the night would belong to it.

Tonight, that feeling was stronger than ever. There was a rustle, a breath, a sound like sandpaper being dragged across stone. Emily clutched her blanket tighter, a whimper escaping her lips. The Boogeyman was there, just beyond the edge of the light.

With a trembling hand, she reached for the small flashlight under her pillow. Its weak beam barely cut into the void, but she felt safer with it—until it flickered. A soft, lilting voice emerged from the closet, neither male nor female, both whisper and roar: "Emily..."

Far above the world, the TARDIS hummed in the vacuum of space, anchored between stars, its deep blue exterior gleaming with a hint of otherworldly life. Inside, the Doctor paced relentlessly, boots echoing on the grating floor as the whir of the console seemed to mirror their restless thoughts. The nightmares had rattled something loose within them, a sense of urgency tangled with foreboding.

Suddenly, a sharp beep from the console snapped the Doctor from their reverie. The monitor flickered, lines of Gallifreyan symbols cascading across the screen before settling into a single, pulsing signal. It was a distress call, faint but undeniable, vibrating with a strange energy that resonated with the lingering remnants of the nightmares.

"Who could it be now?" the Doctor muttered, fingers flying across the controls. The coordinates resolved on the screen: Earth, present-day, a quiet town where nothing extraordinary should be happening. But there, embedded within the mundane transmission, was something older, something that sang of forgotten fears.

The Doctor's expression shifted from curiosity to determination. The nightmares, the whispers in the dark, and now this—a child's plea threaded with an echo of an ancient terror. It was as if the universe itself were pointing the way, pushing them toward a mystery older than any story ever told.

"Hold tight, Emily," the Doctor whispered as the TARDIS engines roared to life, the central column wheezing and pulsing as time and space bent around it. The familiar, haunting groan filled the air, and in an instant, the TARDIS vanished, drawn inexorably toward its next adventure.

The Doctor would soon learn that some monsters do not just lurk in the shadows; they are the shadows. And the Boogeyman was waiting.

Chapter 1: A Mysterious Summons

The TARDIS landed with its characteristic groan and wheeze, the blue police box appearing out of thin air in the middle of a mist-covered park. The trees loomed like skeletal guardians, their gnarled branches tangled with the last remnants of autumn leaves. The Doctor stepped out, adjusting his coat and running a hand through his hair, eyes scanning the surroundings with an intensity that spoke of both excitement and caution.

"Right then, Yaz," the Doctor said, turning to face his companion, Yazmin Khan, who had followed him out with a mix of curiosity and wariness. "Looks like we've got ourselves a proper mystery."

Yaz crossed her arms and gave the Doctor a look that was equal parts exasperation and intrigue. "And by 'proper mystery,' you mean something that'll get us in trouble, don't you?"

The Doctor grinned, the kind of smile that lit up his face and made trouble seem more like an adventure. "Trouble, Yaz, is just the universe's way of saying it needs a bit of attention."

Before Yaz could respond, the sound of hurried footsteps caught their attention. A man, his face pale and eyes wild, stumbled out from behind the thick hedge at the edge of the park. He was dressed in a hastily thrown-on sweater and loose jeans, his hands shaking as he clutched a flashlight. When he saw them, his eyes widened further, filled with a mixture of hope and desperation.

"Are you... police?" he gasped, eyes darting nervously toward the darkened corners of the park.

Yaz stepped forward, showing her badge from her days as an officer. "We're here to help. What's happened?"

"It's my son, Robbie," the man said, the tremor in his voice giving weight to the terror in his eyes. "He disappeared last night. Just vanished without a sound. And... he's not the only one."

The Doctor's expression grew serious. "How many children have gone missing?"

"Three this week," the man whispered, glancing over his shoulder as though expecting something to leap out from the gloom. "And others have been complaining about noises, whispers in the dark, and shadows that move when they shouldn't."

Yaz's brow furrowed. "Has anyone contacted the local authorities?"

The man nodded quickly. "The police don't know what to do. They think it's some kind of sick prank or a runaway case, but I know what I heard last night before Robbie disappeared. There was... there was a voice."

The Doctor's eyes sparked with recognition, a thread connecting in his mind. "A voice, you say? What did it sound like?"

The man's face blanched even further, and he swallowed hard. "It was low, almost like a growl. It called his name, over and over."

The Doctor exchanged a look with Yaz, their expressions grave. "Right, Yaz, I think it's time we did a little exploring."

The man's eyes darted from Yaz to the Doctor, confusion deepening the lines on his face. "Who are you people?"

The Doctor clapped the man on the shoulder reassuringly. "We're the ones who make sure nightmares stay where they belong—locked in the dark." He paused, leaning closer. "Where exactly did your son disappear?"

The man hesitated, then pointed toward a row of houses at the far end of the park, their windows glowing softly in the early evening light. "Our house is just there. But please, whatever you do, be careful."

"Always am," the Doctor said, already striding off, the tails of his coat flaring behind him. Yaz followed, giving the man a quick nod of reassurance before catching up.

The house was modest, its white picket fence casting long shadows under the streetlamp's glow. The Doctor knocked, and a woman opened the door, her eyes red-rimmed and swollen.

"Mr. Johnson said you'd be coming," she whispered, her voice raw with exhaustion and grief. "I'm Sara. Please, come in."

The Doctor and Yaz stepped inside, taking in the living room, which was littered with toys left untouched and a framed family photo that seemed to mock the emptiness in the room. The atmosphere was suffocating, as though the air itself held its breath.

"Mrs. Johnson," the Doctor began, his voice gentle but probing, "can you tell us about last night? Anything strange that happened before Robbie went missing?"

Sara nodded slowly, sinking into the armchair as if her legs could no longer hold her up. "I was putting Robbie to bed. He was restless, said he couldn't sleep because the man in the closet was watching him."

Yaz and the Doctor exchanged a look. "Did he describe this man?" Yaz asked, her voice soft, inviting trust.

Sara wiped at her eyes with a shaking hand. "He said... he said it was dark. Just dark, with eyes that glowed like embers. I didn't think much of it at first. Kids have nightmares. But then, after I tucked him in and went to the kitchen, I heard it. A voice, low and whispering. It called to him, said his name."

A chill swept over the room, tangible and suffocating. The Doctor turned to Yaz, his expression sharpened with the gravity of realization. "We're not dealing with something human. Yaz, this might be exactly what I feared."

Yaz swallowed. "The Boogeyman?"

The Doctor nodded solemnly, then turned back to Sara. "We're going to do everything we can to get Robbie back, I promise you. But I need to ask—has anyone else around here reported hearing voices, seeing anything out of the ordinary?"

Sara's face darkened with the weight of a hidden truth. "Yes. Emily, the girl who lives next door. She told her mother that she saw the shadows moving in her room, and she's been having nightmares about a creature watching her."

The Doctor's eyes narrowed. "Right then. Looks like we'll be paying Emily a visit."

The wind outside rattled the windowpanes as if in agreement, carrying with it an ominous whisper that seemed to echo from somewhere far beyond the edge of the known universe.

"Hold on tight, Yaz," the Doctor murmured as they stepped out into the night. "Things are about to get very dark indeed."

Chapter 2: The Legend of the Boogeyman

The rain had started to fall in a steady drizzle as the Doctor and Yaz walked down the dimly lit main street toward the town's library. The streetlamps cast pools of pale light on the wet pavement, reflecting like ghostly eyes. The town was quiet, too quiet for a place where children had been vanishing without a trace.

The library stood at the end of the street, an imposing building of stone and glass that loomed like a sentinel of forgotten secrets. As they entered, the musty scent of old paper and ink enveloped them, and the creaking of the floorboards announced their presence to an elderly librarian who peered over the top of her thin-rimmed glasses.

"Can I help you?" she asked, her voice thin but steady, eyes sharp and watchful.

The Doctor flashed a wide grin. "Yes! We're looking for any local folklore or legends, particularly about mysterious creatures or disappearances. I believe you might have some books in your mythical section?"

The librarian's brow furrowed. "Folklore, you say? That section doesn't see much attention these days." She pointed a gnarled finger toward the back of the library. "It's down there, last row on the left. Just be careful with the books. Some of them are older than I am."

"Thank you!" Yaz said, giving the woman a polite nod as she followed the Doctor down the narrow aisle. The sound of their footsteps echoed, the dim bulbs overhead casting flickering light across shelves lined with tomes bound in cracked leather and faded cloth.

The Doctor's eyes lit up as he reached the mythical section. The shelves here were dense with forgotten stories—tales that spoke of things that went bump in the night and beings that thrived in the shadows between reality and nightmare. One title immediately caught the Doctor's attention: **The Boogey Book**.

"Ah, look at this," the Doctor said, pulling the heavy tome from its place with care. The cover was embossed with the figure of a twisted silhouette, eyes like pits of flame. The words below read *The Boogey Book: An Account of Fear's Oldest Creature.*

Yaz leaned closer, reading over the Doctor's shoulder. "That's... creepy."

"Creepy doesn't cover half of it," the Doctor murmured, flipping through the yellowed pages. The illustrations were nightmarish, depicting shadowy figures with elongated limbs and jagged teeth. The text was written in an archaic script, yet the Doctor seemed to understand it without effort. "According to this, the Boogeyman isn't just a story used to frighten children. It's a creature that feeds on fear, using it as a portal to abduct its victims into another dimension."

Yaz glanced around as if expecting to see eyes staring out from between the shelves. "Why would it take children, though?"

The Doctor's gaze grew distant, eyes narrowing as they read on. "Children's fear is raw, potent. Unfiltered by the rationalizations that adults use to soothe themselves. It's the perfect fuel for a being that thrives on darkness." He turned a page and frowned. "It says here that these abductions aren't random. The Boogeyman picks children who have witnessed or felt true terror—it's drawn to them, like a moth to a flame."

Yaz shivered despite herself. "So Robbie wasn't the first, and if we don't stop this, he won't be the last."

"Exactly," the Doctor said, slamming the book shut. The sound echoed through the silent library, causing the light above them to flicker momentarily. He placed the book down and reached for another, thinner volume that seemed out of place among the ancient tomes: *The Ultimate Boogeyman Safari.*

"What's that?" Yaz asked, raising an eyebrow at the peculiar title.

The Doctor opened it, revealing pages filled with detailed sketches, eyewitness accounts, and maps marked with strange symbols. "This is like a field guide," the Doctor said, eyebrows shooting up. "It describes various encounters with the Boogeyman across different cultures and times. Some of these sightings date back thousands of years, but what's more intriguing is this." The Doctor pointed to a hastily scribbled note in the margin of one page. It read: *Find the mirrors. They are the key.*

"Mirrors?" Yaz repeated, puzzled.

The Doctor's eyes glinted with understanding. "Of course! Mirrors have often been believed to be portals between worlds, or at least barriers between the real and the unreal. If the Boogeyman is taking children into another dimension, then mirrors might be the way it crosses over."

They were interrupted by the sound of a cough behind them. The elderly librarian stood there, her eyes flickering with a strange light that set the Doctor on edge. "Be careful what you look for, Doctor," she said, her voice low, almost conspiratorial. "The Boogeyman doesn't like to be known. And when you call its name too often, it starts to listen."

Yaz shifted uncomfortably. "Why would you have these books if they're so dangerous?"

The librarian's eyes darkened. "Knowledge is power, and power is the only thing that can keep the darkness at bay. But not all knowledge is safe to wield."

The Doctor's expression hardened. "Don't worry, we're not just wielding knowledge. We're going to use it to fight."

The librarian's lips curled into a faint, weary smile. "Then may the light guide you." She turned and disappeared back down the aisle, leaving them with a silence that felt far too loud.

The Doctor tucked both books under his arm and met Yaz's eyes, the flicker of a plan forming behind his sharp, curious gaze. "Come on, Yaz. We need to pay a visit to Emily and her family. It's time we found out exactly what we're up against."

As they walked out into the night, the rain had stopped, but the chill in the air had deepened. In the shadows cast by the dim streetlights, it was almost as if something moved, watching, waiting.

And somewhere in the heart of the town, in a small, quiet bedroom, a child whispered into the dark, "Please, don't let him come back." But it was too late. The Boogeyman was already listening.

Chapter 3: Into the Darkness

The air in Emily's bedroom was thick with an eerie stillness. The Doctor paused at the threshold, taking in the space. Toys were neatly arranged on shelves, and a small nightlight shaped like a star cast a gentle glow across the room. Yet, despite the child-like innocence of the space, a deep, unsettling tension rippled beneath the surface.

Emily sat on the edge of her bed, clutching a stuffed bear with eyes wide and fearful. Her parents stood in the doorway, watching anxiously as the Doctor moved to the center of the room, his eyes scanning the walls and floor as if reading invisible script. Yaz crouched beside Emily, offering her a reassuring smile.

"Hey, Emily," Yaz said softly, "we're here to help. You're safe now."

Emily's eyes flitted to Yaz's face, then darted quickly to the closet, a door painted white with delicate pink flowers. It stood slightly ajar, an unnatural blackness seeping from the small opening.

"It's there," Emily whispered, voice quivering. "He's in there."

The Doctor's expression darkened as he glanced at the closet. "Right, then. Let's see what we're dealing with." He pulled out the sonic screwdriver, its familiar whir filling the room as he directed the beam toward the closet. The screen flashed erratically, a series of symbols cascading across it that made the Doctor's eyes widen.

"Dark energy residue," he murmured, half to himself. "But this isn't just any dark energy. It's... sentient."

Yaz stood, her brow creased with concern. "Sentient? You mean it's alive?"

The Doctor nodded, not taking his eyes off the device. "Not in the way we understand life, but aware, certainly. It's a signature I haven't seen in centuries. A remnant from the spaces between realities."

Emily's mother, a slender woman with worry carved into every line of her face, stepped forward. "Doctor, what does that mean? Is Emily in danger?"

The Doctor glanced up, his expression softening. "Not if I can help it." He moved to the closet, his fingers brushing the edge of the door. "But I need to know what we're dealing with before we can send it back where it belongs."

He pushed the door open, and the room seemed to draw a collective breath. The darkness inside wasn't just an absence of light; it was an entity in itself, shifting and pulsing with a malevolent will. A chill ran down Yaz's spine as she stared into the abyss.

The Doctor reached into his coat pocket and produced a small, metallic orb. He pressed a button on its surface, and a faint blue light illuminated the closet, casting odd, wavering shadows across the walls.

"Yaz, keep Emily close," the Doctor said, his voice sharp with urgency. "This could get... tricky."

Emily clutched her stuffed bear tighter as Yaz wrapped an arm around her. The room felt colder now, as if an unseen force was drawing the warmth away.

The Doctor stepped into the closet, the blue light revealing swirling patterns along the back wall. It was covered in marks that seemed to shift and writhe like ink in water, forming symbols the Doctor recognized immediately.

"Ancient markings of the Nocturne," he muttered. "Guardians of shadow, hunters of fear."

He turned, eyes locking with Yaz's. "This isn't just a simple abduction, Yaz. The Boogeyman is real, and it's drawing its power from something ancient, something that thrives on terror. These markings... they're part of a gateway."

"A gateway?" Yaz echoed, eyes widening. "To where?"

"To a place where light has no hold, a realm between dimensions where fear feeds on itself until it becomes substance." The Doctor's voice was low, laced with a seriousness that sent shivers down Yaz's spine.

Suddenly, a sound like a whispering wind swept through the room, and the blue light in the Doctor's hand flickered. Emily gasped, burying her face in Yaz's shoulder. The Doctor turned back to the closet, where the darkness seemed to shift, bulging outward as if pressing against an invisible barrier.

A voice, soft and haunting, filled the room. It carried a cadence that made the skin crawl. "You meddle where you shouldn't, Time Lord."

The Doctor's jaw tightened. "Oh, I love it when the monsters know who I am. Makes this dance all the more interesting."

The darkness pulsated, and the whisper came again, closer this time, dripping with venom. "They are mine. You cannot stop me."

"We'll see about that," the Doctor said, adjusting the settings on his sonic screwdriver. The device emitted a high-pitched frequency, and the dark mass in the closet recoiled, its shape distorting like a shadow caught in a windstorm.

Yaz took a step forward, her eyes locked on the Doctor. "What do we do, Doctor? How do we stop it?"

The Doctor turned, the fierce determination in his gaze unwavering. "First, we need to seal this gateway before it has a chance to fully open. Then, we find out how it's anchoring itself here." He looked at Emily, who peeked out from Yaz's embrace. "Emily, have you heard the voice say anything else? Anything important?"

The girl nodded, tears glistening in her eyes. "He says he's coming back. That he'll take me like he took Robbie and the others."

The Doctor's expression darkened. "Then we don't have much time." He stepped back from the closet, the blue orb in his hand glowing brighter as he pressed another button. A series of small, sharp notes echoed out, and the symbols on the closet wall began to glow faintly, the dark energy trembling as if in pain.

With one last pulse of light, the orb released a shockwave that forced the darkness back, sealing the wall with a thin, silvery sheen. The whispering voice faded, leaving the room in heavy silence.

Emily's parents stood frozen, wide-eyed and pale. The Doctor exhaled and turned to Yaz. "That should hold for now, but we need to figure out where this thing is drawing its strength from. Something or someone is feeding it."

Yaz's eyes narrowed as she processed what he was saying. "And we're going to find out, right?"

The Doctor nodded, slipping the orb back into his pocket. "Oh, absolutely. But first, we'll need to speak to the other families. Every piece of information counts when dealing with an entity that calls itself *the Boogeyman.*"

As they left Emily's room, the night outside seemed deeper, the quiet more oppressive. Yaz glanced at the Doctor, seeing the faint worry behind his confident facade.

"We're really in it now, aren't we?" Yaz whispered.

The Doctor's lips curled into a grim smile. "Yes, Yaz. Into the darkness we go."

Chapter 4: Emily's Fear

The small living room of the Johnson household was illuminated by the warm glow of an old lamp. The shadows it cast on the walls felt longer than they should have been, stretching and twisting in ways that made the room feel smaller, more suffocating. Emily sat on the couch, her small hands gripping the edge of her blanket as if it were the only thing tethering her to reality. Her parents stood nearby, watching with a mix of concern and helplessness.

The Doctor knelt down in front of Emily, his eyes softening as he took in her trembling form. Yaz stood beside him, arms crossed, her gaze darting nervously between the child and the hallway that led to the bedrooms.

"Hello, Emily," the Doctor said, his voice warm and calming. "My name's the Doctor, and this is my friend Yaz. We're here to help. Would you mind telling us about the man you see at night?"

Emily's eyes, wide and dark, flickered over to Yaz for reassurance before settling on the Doctor. She nodded slowly and swallowed hard before speaking, her voice so soft it was almost a whisper. "He comes when it's really dark. He waits until Mommy and Daddy are asleep. He... he doesn't come all the way out at first. Just his eyes."

The Doctor's expression grew intense but stayed gentle. "Can you tell me what his eyes look like, Emily?"

Emily shivered, her small frame curling tighter into the blanket. "They're red. Like fire, but cold. And he whispers. I can't understand the words, but it sounds like... like scratching glass."

Yaz glanced at the Doctor, her brows knitted together. "Doctor, that sounds like—"

"—the same description from The Boogey Book," the Doctor finished, nodding. He turned back to Emily, eyes glinting with an odd mixture of curiosity and concern. "And when he comes out, what does he do? Does he move around, or just stand there?"

Emily hesitated, her eyes darting to her mother, who took a small step forward, her face strained. "It's okay, sweetheart. You can tell him."

Emily's lower lip quivered, but she pushed on. "He stands there at first, but then he moves closer. I can't move when he does. It's like I'm stuck. He puts his hand out, like this—" She raised a small, shaking hand toward the Doctor. "—and then I can hear the voice in my head. It's not my voice. It tells me that he's taking me somewhere dark. Somewhere Mommy and Daddy can't find me."

The Doctor's eyes darkened, and he reached out to place a comforting hand on her blanket-covered knee. "Emily, you're very brave for telling me all this. And I promise you, I'm going to make sure he doesn't take you anywhere."

"But how?" Emily's voice broke, tears welling up and spilling over. "He's so strong. I can feel him even when he's not here. He's watching all the time."

The Doctor's eyes softened. "Fear is powerful, Emily. It's what he feeds on. But do you know what's stronger than fear?" He paused, waiting for her to meet his gaze. "Hope. And I've faced creatures like him before. I know how they work, how they think. I won't let him take you."

Emily's tears slowed, a tiny spark of hope lighting in her eyes. "Promise?"

The Doctor's smile was small but resolute. "Cross my hearts."

Yaz's expression remained tense as she shifted her weight. "Doctor, you said he's feeding on fear. If that's the case, Emily and every other kid here are like a buffet to him. How do we stop that?"

The Doctor stood, a thoughtful crease forming between his brows as he began pacing the room. "If he's manifesting through a combination of dark energy and fear, then we need to disrupt the link. Fear acts as an anchor, holding him to this world. But something more is fueling him. We need to find out what."

Emily's father, who had been silent until now, stepped forward. "There's an old tale my grandmother used to tell. She said that shadows can grow stronger when the town's fears align. She called it 'The Gathering Dread.' We always thought it was just a story to keep kids from wandering into the woods at night."

The Doctor's eyes snapped to him, sharp as ever. "The Gathering Dread, you say? Yaz, we may have just found the missing piece of our puzzle. If the town's collective fear is acting as a conduit, then this Boogeyman isn't just feeding on individual fear—he's amplifying it across everyone."

Yaz frowned. "But why now? What's different about this moment that's letting him manifest?"

The Doctor nodded slowly, the gears turning behind his eyes. "Excellent question, Yaz. We need to trace this back to when the disappearances first began, and look for any catalyst. But first, we need to make sure Emily is protected tonight."

Emily's mother's voice trembled as she spoke. "What can we do to keep her safe, Doctor?"

The Doctor pulled a small device from his pocket—a small, round crystal emitting a soft, silver glow. "This is a containment charm, a little piece of alien tech I picked up on a moon where shadows are alive. It won't hold him forever, but it should keep the dark energy at bay long enough for us to find the source and cut him off."

He handed it to Emily's mother, who looked at it as if it were the most precious thing in the world. "Place this in her room tonight, near her bed. It will react if he tries to come through."

Emily's father nodded, his jaw set. "We'll do whatever it takes."

The Doctor leaned in closer to Emily, his expression sincere and determined. "Tonight, you sleep. Let me handle the nightmares."

The little girl nodded, a small, brave smile breaking through the storm of her fear. "Okay, Doctor."

As the night crept closer, the Doctor and Yaz exchanged a final glance. They both knew this was only the beginning, and the Boogeyman was watching, waiting for the moment when the dark would be deep enough for him to return.

Chapter 5: The First Encounter

The Johnson house was cloaked in silence as the night deepened. The entire town seemed to hold its breath, the weight of fear palpable in the stillness. Emily lay in her bed, clutching the small crystal that the Doctor had given her. Its silver glow cast a gentle halo around her, but her eyes kept darting toward the closet, which now seemed larger, darker—hungry.

The Doctor and Yaz stood just outside her room, hidden in the shadowed hallway. The Doctor's eyes were fixed on the thin crack of light under the door, ears attuned to every creak and groan of the old house.

"Do you really think he'll show?" Yaz whispered, her voice barely audible.

The Doctor's jaw tightened, and he nodded once. "He's been waiting for this moment. The more we resist, the more eager he'll be to make himself known. And when he does…" His voice trailed off as he glanced at Yaz. "We'll be ready."

A sudden, bone-chilling gust swept down the hallway, making Yaz shudder. The lights flickered, casting long, dancing shadows. The house seemed to shudder in response, and a faint, metallic scraping sound echoed from behind Emily's door. Yaz's eyes widened, and she reached out instinctively, gripping the Doctor's arm.

"It's starting," she breathed.

The Doctor's eyes narrowed, and he stepped forward, pushing the door open just enough to peer inside. What he saw sent a shiver down even his spine.

A figure stood in the corner of Emily's room, half-hidden by the darkness. It was tall and gaunt, its limbs too long, jointed at unnatural angles. Its face was shrouded in shadows, but its eyes—glowing, deep crimson—burned like embers in a dying fire. The Boogeyman's gaze was fixed on Emily, who lay frozen with fear, eyes wide and glistening with unshed tears.

The Doctor pushed the door open fully and stepped inside, his sonic screwdriver already in his hand. "That's far enough!" he called, his voice strong, unyielding.

The Boogeyman's head jerked up, and a sound like nails on a chalkboard filled the room. The corners of its mouth stretched into a grotesque grin, revealing rows of jagged, yellow teeth. "Time Lord," it whispered, the word slithering from its lips like a curse. "You dare to interfere."

Yaz stepped in behind the Doctor, heart pounding as the figure's eyes flicked to her. She swallowed hard but stood her ground, fists clenched at her sides.

"You're not taking her," the Doctor said, his tone cold as steel. He raised the sonic screwdriver, and its blue light whirred, casting a bright, pulsating glow that pushed the shadows back. The Boogeyman recoiled, its form rippling as if made of smoke.

The creature let out a low, guttural laugh that resonated in their bones. "You think a toy can banish me? You know nothing of the dark. You meddle in forces you cannot comprehend."

The Doctor's eyes narrowed. "Try me," he said, stepping closer, the sonic screwdriver humming in warning.

The Boogeyman's crimson eyes flared, and the room seemed to grow colder. Emily let out a small gasp as the crystal in her hand flared brighter, fighting against the dark energy that pressed in around her. The creature raised one long, clawed hand, pointing a talon-like finger at the Doctor.

"This town's fear has made me strong, Time Lord. You cannot stop what has already begun. I will feast on their terror until I am reborn."

"Not if I have anything to say about it," the Doctor replied, pressing a button on the sonic screwdriver. A high-pitched frequency filled the room, and the Boogeyman let out a shriek, its form distorting as the light from the crystal joined in, a brilliant silver glow pushing the shadow back.

Yaz stepped forward, voice steady despite the fear gnawing at her insides. "You heard the Doctor. Get out."

The Boogeyman's form wavered, its grin faltering as the combined force of the sonic and the crystal's energy pushed it back toward the closet. But before it faded entirely, it snarled, eyes locking onto the Doctor with a look of pure malice.

"You cannot stop the darkness," it hissed. "I will return, and when I do, there will be no corner of your precious universe that is safe from me."

With a final, shuddering pulse, the Boogeyman was gone. The room fell silent, the temperature slowly rising back to normal. Emily let out a small sob of relief as Yaz rushed to her side, wrapping her arms around the trembling girl.

The Doctor's eyes lingered on the closet, now just a piece of furniture again, its menace hidden but not forgotten. He slipped the sonic screwdriver back into his coat and turned to Yaz and Emily.

"Are you alright?" he asked softly.

Emily nodded, the tears finally spilling down her cheeks. "I was so scared," she whispered.

The Doctor crouched down, meeting her eyes. "You were brave, Emily. Braver than most adults would be. And I meant what I said—I'll make sure he never comes back."

Yaz met the Doctor's eyes, worry etched into her face. "Doctor, he said he's feeding on the whole town's fear. How do we stop that?"

The Doctor straightened, his expression serious. "We find out what's fueling him and cut it off at the source. But it won't be easy. Whatever's anchoring him here has roots deep in this town's history. We need to dig deeper."

As they left Emily's room, the Doctor paused for a moment, glancing back at the closet. The Boogeyman's warning echoed in his mind: *You cannot stop the darkness.* A chill ran down his spine, but he pushed it aside. There was work to be done, and time was not on their side.

"Come on, Yaz," he said, his voice firm. "We're going to need every ounce of courage we have for what comes next."

Chapter 6: The Dimension of Shadows

The morning sun cast long beams of light across the Johnsons' living room, but the warm glow felt hollow. The entire house seemed steeped in an unshakeable tension. Emily was asleep now, exhausted from the terror of the night before. Her parents sat in the kitchen, whispering anxiously, while Yaz paced the floor, casting glances at the Doctor who was hunched over the coffee table, surrounded by books and notes hastily scrawled in Gallifreyan script.

The Doctor's brow was furrowed in concentration as he read through an ancient tome he had taken from the library—*The Boogey Book*. Pages filled with arcane symbols and chilling illustrations of shadowy figures flipped under his fingers. Beside it lay *The Ultimate Boogeyman Safari*, with pages marked by hastily scribbled notes. He paused, eyes narrowing as he traced a particular line with his finger.

"It's not just folklore," he muttered, almost to himself. "It's a map."

Yaz paused mid-stride, her eyes narrowing. "A map? What do you mean, Doctor?"

The Doctor glanced up, eyes alight with discovery. "The stories, the symbols—it all points to a realm that exists parallel to our own. A dark dimension, a place without light, where fear isn't just an emotion but a source of sustenance. The Boogeyman isn't from here; he's an interloper from this Dimension of Shadows."

Yaz's jaw tensed as she processed his words. "So, he's not just some supernatural creature. He's an invader."

"Exactly!" The Doctor's eyes gleamed. "And if he's feeding off the town's collective fear, that means there's an opening between our dimension and his. A weak spot that he's using to cross over."

A heavy silence settled between them as the implications sank in. Yaz broke it, voice firm. "If there's an opening, we can find it and shut it down, right?"

The Doctor leaned back, running a hand through his hair. "Not quite that simple, Yaz. This type of rift doesn't just close. It's like a wound that needs to be healed from both sides. We'd have to enter the Dimension of Shadows, find the source of his power, and sever it from within."

Yaz's eyes widened. "Enter the dimension? You mean, we'd have to go into *his* world? Doctor, that's madness."

"Madness, yes," the Doctor admitted, a small, wry smile tugging at the corner of his lips. "But it's also the only way. We can't just play defense; we need to go on the offensive."

Before Yaz could respond, Emily's father, Mr. Johnson, appeared in the doorway. He had been listening, his face pale. "You mean to say you're planning to go into that... that thing's world? How? And why?"

The Doctor stood, eyes resolute. "Because it's the only way to stop him from coming back. If we don't, more children will vanish, more families will be torn apart. I can't let that happen."

Mr. Johnson's eyes glistened with fear and hope. "But how can you even open a portal to a place like that? It sounds... impossible."

The Doctor's smile broadened. "Oh, impossible is my favorite kind of challenge." He walked to the TARDIS, which hummed quietly in the corner of the room, disguised as an old wardrobe. He placed a hand on its cool surface. "This old girl can bridge the gap between worlds. But it's not just a simple jump. I'll need a source of fear strong enough to amplify the TARDIS's power and pinpoint the rift."

Yaz's eyes lit up with understanding. "The town's fear. That's why he's here—he needs it. If we use it, we can find where he's anchored."

"Precisely!" The Doctor clapped his hands together, already spinning into action. "But it's not without risks. The Dimension of Shadows isn't bound by the rules of our world. Time and space twist and break there. We need to be ready for anything."

Mr. Johnson stepped forward, fists clenching. "But how do you make sure you come back? If it's so dangerous, how do we know you won't get trapped?"

The Doctor's face softened. "There's always a risk. But that's why Yaz and I have to be prepared for every contingency. We'll create an anchor point in the TARDIS so that if the worst happens, it will pull us back."

Yaz nodded, determination in her eyes. "So, what's the plan? How do we start?"

The Doctor's eyes gleamed with intensity. "We'll use the energy residue in Emily's room. It's where the rift is strongest. I'll configure the TARDIS to amplify the fear energy and focus it like a beacon. That should open a portal, just long enough for us to step through."

Mr. Johnson looked at his daughter, still asleep, and then back at the Doctor. His voice was hoarse, barely holding back a plea. "Just... promise me you'll bring her peace. End this nightmare."

The Doctor stepped forward and placed a hand on Mr. Johnson's shoulder. "I promise. This ends tonight."

The TARDIS interior was awash with light as the Doctor manipulated the console, adjusting levers and twisting dials with practiced precision. Yaz stood to one side, watching the readings spike on the monitor as the old ship hummed with a deep, resonant power.

The Doctor looked up at her, eyes sharp and determined. "Yaz, once we step through, everything will change. The Dimension of Shadows isn't just a place—it's a living entity. It will try to trick you, show you your worst fears. You need to stay focused."

Yaz nodded, swallowing hard. "I'm with you, Doctor. Whatever happens, we face it together."

A faint tremor passed through the floor, and the console screen lit up with swirling, dark patterns that mirrored the ones they had seen in Emily's closet. The TARDIS emitted a deep, thrumming sound as the walls seemed to stretch and warp.

"Hold on!" the Doctor shouted as a brilliant, silvery tear opened in the center of the room. The light shifted, folding in on itself until it became a gaping portal of darkness that pulsed with an unnatural energy.

Yaz's breath caught in her throat as a chilling voice echoed from within the tear, a voice that sent a shiver down her spine. "Come, Time Lord. Face me where the shadows dance."

The Doctor's eyes flared with defiance as he stepped forward, the hum of the TARDIS surrounding him like an invisible shield. He glanced at Yaz, a spark of camaraderie passing between them.

"Ready?" he asked, his voice steady.

Yaz took a deep breath and nodded. "Ready."

And with that, they stepped through the portal, into the heart of darkness where fear reigned supreme.

Chapter 7: The Missing Children

The transition into the Dimension of Shadows was not like any journey Yaz had experienced before. The sensation was disorienting, like falling and flying simultaneously. Darkness enveloped them, pressing in with a weight that made it difficult to breathe. When their feet found solid ground, the Doctor and Yaz found themselves standing on a landscape that defied logic.

The ground beneath them was dark and shifting, made of a material that seemed to pulse with an eerie, liquid-like quality. The sky was an endless expanse of black, speckled with tendrils of shadow that writhed and moved as though alive. Everything was bathed in a dim, unnatural glow, casting warped, twisting shadows.

"Doctor," Yaz whispered, her voice taut with unease, "what is this place?"

The Doctor's face was grim, eyes scanning their surroundings as he kept the sonic screwdriver in a tight grip. "This is the Dimension of Shadows, Yaz. A realm between realities where the very air is steeped in fear. It's where the Boogeyman draws his power, and where he keeps those he's taken."

A soft, echoing sound like the faint cry of a child reached their ears. Yaz's heart clenched as she turned toward it, eyes searching the shadowed horizon. "Did you hear that?"

The Doctor nodded, his expression hardening. "Yes, and we need to move fast. Time doesn't work the same way here. What's been days for us might have been years for them—or only minutes. We can't be sure."

Yaz's eyes darkened with determination. "Then let's go. We have to find them."

They moved forward cautiously, each step making the ground ripple beneath their feet. The landscape was labyrinthine, with towering spires of shadow that twisted and contorted, forming corridors that shifted when they weren't looking. The cries grew louder, more distinct, filling the space with an unsettling chorus of lost voices.

Suddenly, a figure darted past them—a flash of small, pale limbs and wide, frightened eyes. Yaz gasped, reaching out instinctively. "Wait! Come back!"

The child paused, turning with a face that was streaked with tears and dirt. It was Robbie, Mr. Johnson's son. His eyes were filled with a fear that was almost primal. "He's coming," he whispered, voice trembling. "He's always coming."

The Doctor crouched down, his face softening. "Robbie, it's okay. We're here to take you home. Where are the others?"

Robbie's eyes darted around, as if he expected the darkness itself to snatch him away. "They're hiding. We tried to run, but he always finds us."

Yaz stepped closer, keeping her voice calm and soothing. "Where are they now, Robbie? We need to find them."

Robbie pointed toward a cluster of shadowy pillars that twisted like ancient trees. "In there. But it's not safe."

The Doctor's jaw set, and he exchanged a quick glance with Yaz. "We're going in. Robbie, stay close to Yaz. Don't let go of her hand, no matter what happens."

Robbie nodded, small fingers reaching out to clutch Yaz's hand like a lifeline. She squeezed back reassuringly, even as the chill of the realm sent a shiver down her spine.

They approached the cluster of spires, their forms shifting and groaning as though aware of their presence. The Doctor raised the sonic screwdriver and activated it, the high-pitched whir cutting through the oppressive silence. The spires recoiled slightly, their surfaces undulating like living tissue.

"Come on, come on," the Doctor muttered, his eyes scanning the space between the pillars. The shadows seemed to grow denser, resisting their passage.

A voice, deep and mocking, echoed through the realm, shaking the ground beneath their feet. "You dare trespass in my domain, Time Lord?"

Yaz's grip on Robbie tightened as she glanced around, searching for the source. The Doctor's expression was fierce, undaunted. "Yes, and I'm here to take back what you stole."

A low, rumbling laugh filled the air, sending a wave of dread through them. "They are mine. Their fear feeds me, gives me life. You cannot steal what is bound by terror."

The Doctor's eyes narrowed. "That's where you're wrong. Fear may have brought you power, but hope will undo you." He raised the screwdriver, and a pulse of energy shot out, slicing through the shadows like a knife. For a brief moment, the darkness parted, revealing a hidden space within the spires.

Huddled together were a dozen children, their faces pale and eyes wide with a mixture of hope and terror. Emily was among them, clutching another child's hand and staring at the Doctor and Yaz as though they were a miracle come to life.

"Emily!" Yaz called, relief flooding her voice.

Emily's eyes lit up, and she scrambled to her feet, pulling the other children with her. "You came! You found us!"

The Doctor moved quickly, waving them forward. "We're getting you all out of here. Stay close and follow me. This place will fight to keep you, but you have to stay brave."

Robbie's small voice quivered. "He's coming. He'll be angry."

A shadow detached from the darkness, forming into the gaunt, towering figure of the Boogeyman. His eyes glowed with an unnatural crimson light, and his mouth stretched into a grin that was all sharp angles and malice.

"You will not leave," the Boogeyman growled, the words reverberating in the air like thunder. "This place is mine, and so are they."

The Doctor's face was a mask of defiance as he stepped between the Boogeyman and the children. "You may rule the shadows, but you do not rule them. I do."

The Boogeyman lunged, a mass of shadow and claws, but the Doctor's sonic screwdriver erupted in a brilliant burst of energy. The creature screamed, the sound splitting the air as it staggered back, momentarily weakened.

"Yaz, now!" the Doctor shouted.

Yaz ushered the children forward, pushing them toward the shifting rift that the TARDIS had created as their way back. One by one, the children leapt into the light, their small bodies disappearing from the realm of darkness.

The Boogeyman's eyes flared, and he reached out with long, clawed hands. "No! You cannot take them from me!"

The Doctor took a step back, eyes meeting the creature's with an unwavering stare. "Oh, but I just did."

As the last child disappeared through the rift, the Boogeyman lunged again, but the Doctor spun, grabbing Yaz's hand and pulling her into the light. The realm screamed around them, a cacophony of rage and loss, as the portal snapped shut behind them.

They stumbled out of the TARDIS and back into Emily's bedroom. The air was thick with relief and the sounds of children crying out in joy as they clung to their parents. Robbie's father fell to his knees, wrapping his arms around his son as tears streamed down his face. Emily's mother held her daughter close, whispering thanks over and over.

Yaz exhaled shakily, leaning against the wall as she watched the scene unfold. The Doctor stood in the middle of it all, eyes scanning the room as though he could still feel the echoes of the dark realm pressing against reality.

"We did it, Doctor," Yaz said, voice barely above a whisper.

The Doctor's eyes met hers, and a small smile broke through the tension. "Yes, Yaz. But this was only one battle. There will always be shadows lurking, waiting for the chance to cross over."

Yaz nodded, understanding the unspoken warning. "But they'll have to get through us first."

The Doctor's grin widened, full of pride and determination. "Exactly."

The Boogeyman had been defeated, the children saved, but as the Doctor looked out into the quiet night beyond the window, he knew that the battle against the dark would never truly end. And as long as there was light, he would be there to keep it burning.

Chapter 8: The Shadow Trap

The town's quiet streets were lined with the remnants of fallen leaves, the crisp autumn air laced with the sense of uneasy calm. Parents kept their children close, eyes flickering nervously as whispers spread through the small community about the miraculous return of their lost children. But the darkness had not left; it lingered like a storm on the horizon, waiting to unleash itself again.

In the center of town, the Doctor and Yaz stood in an old, abandoned schoolhouse. The building had been chosen carefully—it was isolated, made of strong, timeworn stone, and held a certain air of resilience. Inside, the Doctor worked with feverish intensity, setting up devices that hummed and glowed with an otherworldly light. The room was dimly lit, casting long shadows that writhed as if alive.

Yaz watched as the Doctor adjusted a small, circular device that emitted a pulsing blue glow. "Are you sure this will work?" she asked, her voice low, eyes darting around the shadow-streaked corners.

The Doctor looked up, his eyes alight with determination. "It has to. This device will mimic the fear signatures the Boogeyman feeds on. Once it senses the energy, it will be drawn here, and then we'll be able to observe it—under controlled conditions."

Yaz crossed her arms, an uneasy frown etching her face. "Controlled conditions in an abandoned schoolhouse? I wouldn't exactly call that safe."

The Doctor flashed her a quick, reassuring smile. "Ah, but that's where the brilliance comes in. The sonic frequency emitters are positioned around the room. When triggered, they'll create a containment field. It won't hold him forever, but it'll be long enough for me to study his weaknesses."

Yaz nodded, though a chill ran down her spine at the thought of facing the creature again. The memory of its crimson eyes and bone-chilling voice still haunted her. "And what if it breaks through?"

The Doctor's smile faltered for just a moment before returning, more forced this time. "Then we run. Fast."

A sudden, deep silence filled the room, as if the air itself had been sucked away. The lights flickered, and the temperature dropped abruptly. The Doctor straightened, eyes narrowing as he glanced at Yaz. "It's coming."

The shadows along the walls deepened, slithering together to form a dense, amorphous mass. It pulsed, shifting until a familiar figure emerged—tall, gaunt, eyes glowing with the red light of malevolence. The Boogeyman stood before them, its grin wide and jagged.

"Time Lord," it drawled, the sound scraping against their minds like claws on stone. "You set a trap for the dark? Foolish."

The Doctor held his ground, the sonic screwdriver buzzing in his hand. "Yes, well, I do like a challenge. Care to tell me why you're so drawn to this town? Why now?"

The Boogeyman tilted its head, the movement unsettlingly fluid. "The fear here is ripe, a harvest long awaited. Decades of whispered legends, fear passed down from parents to children, feeding the ground until it called to me."

Yaz's eyes widened. "So it's the town itself? The stories, the fear—they've been building up for years."

The creature's eyes flicked to her, and the air thickened with a sudden, suffocating pressure. "Clever little humans. But knowledge will not save you."

The Doctor activated the containment field with a flick of his wrist, and a shimmering, blue-tinted barrier snapped into place around the Boogeyman. The creature flinched, eyes narrowing as it tested the barrier with a swipe of its long, clawed hand. The field rippled but held.

"Excellent," the Doctor muttered, adjusting the settings on the sonic screwdriver. "Now, let's see what you're made of."

The Boogeyman's grin disappeared, replaced by a snarl. "You think this prison will hold me? Fear binds me to this world, and fear has no boundaries."

The barrier quaked, a low hum vibrating through the floor as the shadow figure expanded, pressing against the field with a force that made the Doctor's eyes widen. The lights flickered, and the room darkened as a wave of palpable fear washed over them, stronger than anything they'd felt before.

Yaz's breath came in short, sharp gasps as the air around her seemed to close in. "Doctor, it's breaking through!"

The Doctor's hands moved in a blur as he recalibrated the emitters. "Hold on, Yaz. Just a little longer." Beads of sweat formed on his brow as the field shimmered, cracks of shadow seeping through like ink in water.

The Boogeyman's eyes blazed, and its voice dropped to a whisper that slithered through the room. "You cannot contain the dark, Doctor. It has always existed, waiting in the hearts of those who fear it."

With a final, earsplitting crack, the containment field shattered. The Boogeyman surged forward, shadowy limbs unfurling like tendrils toward Yaz. The Doctor sprang into action, thrusting the sonic screwdriver toward the creature and emitting a burst of energy that slowed its advance, if only for a moment.

"Yaz, get behind me!" the Doctor shouted.

She stumbled back, her eyes wide with a mix of terror and defiance. "What now, Doctor?"

He met her gaze, the weight of realization in his eyes. "We need to change the game. This isn't just about studying its weaknesses—it's about finding a way to sever its connection to fear."

The Boogeyman roared, the sound a chorus of wails and cries that resonated in their bones. It lunged, but the Doctor was quicker, pressing a button on his device that sent a wave of concentrated light crashing into the creature. It recoiled, hissing as the light burned through its form.

"Fear is your weapon," the Doctor said, voice steady despite the chaos around him. "But hope is stronger. And as long as there's a single person willing to fight, you won't win."

The Boogeyman's eyes narrowed, and it began to dissolve back into the shadows, its voice echoing as it retreated. "This is not the end, Time Lord. The darkness will rise again, and when it does, you will be powerless to stop it."

As the last vestige of the creature vanished, the room stilled, the silence heavy and suffocating. Yaz collapsed against the wall, chest heaving as she tried to catch her breath.

The Doctor moved to her side, eyes full of concern. "Are you alright?"

She nodded weakly, wiping the sweat from her brow. "That was too close, Doctor. It's stronger than we thought."

The Doctor's gaze drifted to the shattered containment field, a shadow of worry crossing his features. "Yes, Yaz. It is. But now we know its secret—fear binds it to this world. If we can break that connection, we might just stand a chance."

Yaz met his eyes, the flicker of hope lighting within her exhaustion. "Then let's figure out how to do that. Before it comes back."

The Doctor nodded, determination solidifying in his gaze. The battle was far from over, but they had taken their first step in understanding the true nature of the Boogeyman. And as long as they held onto hope, they had a fighting chance.

Chapter 9: Facing Fears

The morning after their harrowing encounter with the Boogeyman, the Doctor and Yaz sat in the TARDIS. The central console hummed softly, casting a gentle glow that contrasted with the tension crackling between them. The Doctor moved with practiced urgency, adjusting dials and monitoring energy readings, while Yaz sat on a bench, staring at her hands.

The memory of the Boogeyman's gaze lingered, its voice slithering through her mind like a serpent. She shivered involuntarily, a wave of unease tightening her chest. The Doctor glanced at her, his brow furrowing.

"Yaz, you're too quiet. What's going on in that head of yours?" The Doctor's voice was gentle but probing.

Yaz didn't meet his eyes, her voice barely a whisper. "It's nothing. Just... last night was intense. That's all."

The Doctor stopped what he was doing and walked over, sitting across from her. He leaned forward, eyes searching hers. "We've faced plenty of intense moments, Yaz. This is different. Talk to me."

She looked up, eyes haunted. "When it attacked, Doctor, I felt... paralyzed. It wasn't just the fear of the Boogeyman. It was something deeper. Something from when I was a kid." She hesitated, swallowing hard. "I've never told anyone this, but when I was little, I used to see things in the shadows. Figures that whispered my name. I thought it was just my imagination, but now..."

The Doctor's eyes softened with understanding. "The Boogeyman taps into those deep-rooted fears. It finds the cracks in our minds and pushes until we break. It's using that fear against you."

Yaz looked away, her hands trembling slightly. "When it looked at me, I felt like that scared little girl again, hiding under the covers and hoping the voices would stop. What if I can't fight it, Doctor? What if it takes me?"

The Doctor reached out and placed a firm but reassuring hand on her shoulder. "Listen to me, Yaz. Fear is powerful, yes. But it's not invincible. It only wins if we let it control us. You've faced down alien war-lords, weeping angels, and intergalactic storms. You've stood by my side through dangers most people can't even imagine. You're stronger than this."

A flicker of doubt crossed her face, quickly replaced by a determined glint. "I want to believe that, but how do I fight something that knows me so well? Something that *is* fear?"

The Doctor's expression turned serious, a mix of compassion and re-solve. "We face it together. But first, you need to confront what it's us-ing against you. We need to go back, to that moment when you first felt the fear. Only by facing it head-on can you break its hold on you."

Yaz's breath caught in her throat. The thought of revisiting those dark nights from her childhood made her feel cold. But she nodded, a shaky resolve settling in her chest. "Alright. Let's do it."

The Doctor had set the TARDIS to simulate Yaz's childhood bed-room, using the remnants of her memories to recreate every detail. Yaz walked in, her eyes scanning the familiar setting—the small bed with its well-worn quilt, the old posters on the walls, and the bookshelf filled with dog-eared stories. The air felt heavy, and the shadows in the corners seemed deeper, almost sentient.

The Doctor stood by the door, observing her. "It's just a room, Yaz. But your mind is powerful. It will fill in the blanks."

She nodded slowly, moving to sit on the edge of the bed. The creak of the mattress sent a shiver down her spine. The memories were sharp now, clawing their way back to the surface. The feeling of lying awake at night, holding her breath as she heard the faintest whisper of her name coming from the dark.

"Yaz..."

She froze. The voice, thin and echoing, drifted from the shadowed corner of the room. Her heart pounded in her chest as she turned her head slowly, eyes locked on the darkness. It felt real. Too real.

The Doctor stepped closer, his voice low and steady. "Remember, Yaz. It's not real. It's a manifestation of your fear. You control it."

The shadows shifted, a figure forming with eyes like burning coals. It took a step forward, the whisper turning into a growl. "You can't hide from me."

Yaz's breath quickened, memories crashing over her in a torrent. She was a child again, vulnerable and small, wishing for the safety of the morning light. But then she felt the Doctor's presence beside her, grounding her in the present.

"You're not that little girl anymore, Yaz," he said, his voice unwavering. "You're a warrior, a protector. This thing doesn't define you."

The shadow took another step forward, and Yaz stood up, her legs trembling. She clenched her fists, her voice shaking but strong. "You don't control me. Not anymore."

The shadow paused, flickering like a dying flame. The Doctor smiled softly, pride shining in his eyes. "Good. Now show it what happens when you fight back."

Yaz took a deep breath, focusing on the fear that had gripped her for so long. She spoke with a voice filled with defiance. "You're just a shadow. You only have power if I let you."

The shadow let out a low hiss, but it began to recede, its form disintegrating into wisps of dark smoke that vanished into the corners of the room. The oppressive feeling lifted, replaced by a lightness that Yaz hadn't felt in years. She exhaled shakily, a smile breaking through as tears filled her eyes.

The Doctor clapped a hand on her shoulder, his smile broad. "Well done, Yaz. You faced your fear, and you won."

She turned to him, wiping her eyes. "I didn't do it alone."

"No," the Doctor agreed, his eyes warm. "But you had the strength all along. Remember that."

A sudden noise, like a distant echo of laughter, interrupted the moment. The Doctor's expression darkened as he glanced around. "The Boogeyman felt that. It's weakened, but it knows we're coming for it."

Yaz straightened, a newfound confidence in her stance. "Good. Let it know. We're not afraid anymore."

The Doctor's eyes sparkled with determination. "Exactly. And now, it's time to take the fight to the shadows."

Chapter 10: Journey to the Boogey World

The TARDIS thrummed with an energy that was palpable, the golden light from the central column flickering with an intensity that spoke of the gravity of their mission. The Doctor moved around the console with sharp, precise motions, flipping switches and turning dials. The time rotor pumped steadily, but the usual rhythmic hum had a deeper, almost ominous note to it.

Emily stood next to Yaz, clutching the fabric of Yaz's jacket as her wide eyes darted around the alien interior. She had only just recovered from her ordeal, but now, at the Doctor's insistence, she was back inside the TARDIS, facing the nightmare that had haunted her nights.

Yaz knelt beside her, voice low and gentle. "Emily, I know this is scary, but we need your help. You're braver than you know, and the Doctor and I won't let anything happen to you."

Emily nodded, her small face set with determination beyond her years. "I don't want him to hurt anyone else."

The Doctor turned to them, his expression fierce but compassionate. "That's the spirit, Emily. Now, both of you, hold tight. We're about to cross into a place where fear isn't just a feeling—it's a force."

The TARDIS shuddered as if in protest, the lights dimming momentarily before a surge of energy pulsed through the room. The Doctor glanced at the monitor, which displayed a swirling mass of shadow and light, a tear in the fabric of reality.

"Here we go," he muttered, pulling a lever that sent the ship lurching forward. The sound of the engines groaning filled the air, and the floor beneath their feet vibrated as the TARDIS pushed through the thin barrier between worlds.

The transition was sudden and jarring. The usual thrum of the TARDIS fell silent, replaced by a deep, unnatural hum that resonated in their bones. The doors opened of their own accord, revealing a landscape that defied comprehension.

Yaz stepped forward, her breath catching in her throat. "What... what is this place?"

The Doctor walked past her, eyes scanning the scene with both awe and apprehension. "Welcome to the Boogey World, Yaz. A realm where fear shapes reality."

They stepped out into a world that twisted and pulsed as if alive. The ground was an expanse of dark, slick material that rippled with each step, like a pool of black water suspended in time. The sky—or what passed for a sky—was a churning void of deep purples and blacks, with streaks of crimson lightning that cracked soundlessly, illuminating grotesque silhouettes that slithered across the horizon.

Emily gasped as shapes began to form out of the shadows—tall, thin figures with hollow eyes that seemed to move just out of sight. One of them shifted and craned its head toward the group, eyes glowing with a familiar, malicious light.

"It's him," Emily whispered, her voice trembling.

The Doctor nodded, his gaze steely. "Not just him, Emily. This place is an extension of his will, a world built from the fears he's harvested."

Yaz's fingers tightened around her flashlight, the beam of light shaking as it caught a glistening figure moving in the periphery. "Doctor, how do we fight an entire world?"

The Doctor took a deep breath, eyes flicking to Emily. "We don't fight it, Yaz. We confront it. We're here to find the heart of this place—where the Boogeyman draws his power. If we can sever that connection, we break his hold on our world."

The ground beneath them rippled as if responding to the Doctor's words. A low, guttural sound echoed through the space, a laugh that vibrated in their chests. The Boogeyman emerged from the shifting darkness, taller and more grotesque than before. His eyes were burning coals set deep in a face that seemed to change shape, flickering between a skull and a monstrous grin.

"Foolish Time Lord," the Boogeyman said, his voice a mix of a growl and a hiss. "You bring your fear to my domain? You feed me willingly."

The Doctor stepped forward, his gaze never wavering. "I brought something more powerful than fear—hope. And that, my friend, is something you'll never understand."

The Boogeyman's grin faltered, eyes narrowing. "Hope is fleeting. Fear is eternal."

As the creature spoke, the ground beneath their feet began to shift, twisting into jagged, obsidian spikes that shot up like teeth from a gaping maw. Yaz grabbed Emily, pulling her back as the spikes missed them by inches. The Doctor activated his sonic screwdriver, a high-pitched hum resonating through the air and pushing the advancing shadows back for a moment.

"Move!" the Doctor shouted, leading them toward a narrow path that snaked through the chaotic landscape. The path shifted beneath them, twisting like a living thing as the Boogeyman's laughter filled the void.

The trio ran, Emily's small legs moving as fast as they could manage. The world around them shifted, illusions forming and dissipating in the blink of an eye—flashes of the children's rooms, the Johnsons' home, and other twisted memories designed to sap their will.

Emily stopped abruptly, her eyes wide with horror as she pointed to a figure standing in the distance. It was herself, a mirror image, pale and trembling. The doppelgänger spoke, its voice an echo. "You're too weak. You'll never beat him."

Yaz knelt beside Emily, gripping her shoulders. "Don't listen to it. It's not real. You're stronger than this. You faced him before, and you're facing him now."

Emily's lip trembled, but she nodded, eyes shining with determination. The illusion flickered and shattered, the Boogeyman's frustrated roar splitting the air.

"You think you can defy me here, in my world?" he growled, advancing with shadowy limbs that twisted like serpents.

The Doctor stepped in front of Yaz and Emily, his voice booming with a mix of anger and defiance. "This world isn't yours. It's made of fear, yes, but it's also made of the memories and hopes of those you've tried to break. And that's where you've lost."

He held up a device—a small, glowing sphere that pulsed with a light that seemed to repel the encroaching darkness. The Boogeyman's eyes widened, and he recoiled, the ground trembling beneath them.

"What is that?" Yaz shouted over the rumbling.

The Doctor grinned, eyes alight with triumph. "A little piece of home. A stabilizer infused with the hope and bravery of those who fought before us." He turned to Emily. "Emily, this is your chance. You need to be brave, just one more time. Tell him he has no power here."

The Boogeyman shrieked, his form splintering as if the world around him was fighting against his will. Emily took a step forward, small fists clenched, and shouted with a voice full of defiance and fearlessness. "You don't control me. You don't control any of us!"

A wave of light burst from the sphere, spreading outward and cutting through the shadows like a blade. The Boogeyman howled, his form shattering into shards of darkness that dissolved into the air. The world around them began to quake, the churning sky splitting as light flooded in, dispelling the remaining shadows.

The Doctor grabbed Yaz and Emily's hands as the TARDIS doors appeared in front of them, bathed in the warm, golden glow of safety. "Time to go home!" he shouted, pulling them through as the Boogey World disintegrated behind them.

The TARDIS doors slammed shut, and the hum of its engines roared to life. The three of them collapsed to the floor, breaths ragged and hearts racing. For a moment, there was only silence, the weight of victory settling over them.

Yaz sat up, a smile breaking through her exhaustion. "We did it."

The Doctor leaned back against the console, eyes closed, a small smile on his lips. "Yes, Yaz. And now, he's gone. For good."

Emily sat between them, her face bright with relief. "Thank you, Doctor. Thank you for everything."

The Doctor's eyes opened, full of warmth and pride. "No, Emily. Thank *you*. You showed us that even in the darkest places, the light of courage can shine the brightest."

As the TARDIS hummed in gentle victory, the Boogeyman's world faded from existence, and peace returned to the town, no longer bound by the chains of fear.

Chapter 11: Trapped in the Boogey World

The TARDIS shuddered violently as it passed through the rift, the familiar thrum of its engines echoing with an unsettling resonance. Yaz clutched the railing, eyes wide as the walls of the console room flickered between their familiar coral design and an inky blackness that seeped through the seams like tendrils of liquid night.

"Doctor, what's happening?" Yaz shouted over the cacophony of groaning metal and the unsettling hiss that filled the air.

The Doctor, jaw set and eyes blazing with determination, flicked switches and twisted dials in rapid succession. "We're caught in a feedback loop! The Boogey World doesn't want us here, but it's also trying to keep us. It's trapping us in a web of nightmares."

Emily huddled close to Yaz, her small fingers digging into Yaz's sleeve. "I don't like this. It feels... wrong."

The TARDIS lurched again, and suddenly, the noise stopped. An unnatural silence filled the space, thick and suffocating. The Doctor glanced around, brow furrowed, before stepping away from the console.

"Stay close," he said, voice low. "This is where things get tricky."

They approached the doors cautiously. The Doctor took a deep breath and pushed them open, revealing the same nightmarish landscape they had glimpsed before—a world built from the darkest corners of the mind.

The ground rippled under their feet, a slick, viscous substance that made walking a challenge. The sky was an abyssal black, crisscrossed with veins of crimson lightning that illuminated the grotesque shapes writhing just beyond sight. Shadows moved independently of any light source, skittering and slithering like living things.

Yaz swallowed hard. "This place is alive, Doctor. It's like it's watching us."

The Doctor nodded, eyes scanning the horizon for any sign of the missing children. "It is. This realm feeds on fear, shapes itself around it. The more afraid we are, the stronger it becomes. We need to keep our wits about us."

A sudden, high-pitched giggle echoed around them, and Emily flinched, eyes darting to the side. A small, shadowy figure emerged from the dark, its form twisting and flickering as it moved. It looked like a child, but its eyes were hollow, voids of darkness that seemed to pull in all light.

"Play with us," it whispered, voice overlapping as if spoken by many children at once. More figures appeared, circling the group with unsettling smiles and outstretched hands.

Emily's grip on Yaz tightened, and Yaz forced herself to stay calm, even as a chill ran down her spine. "Doctor, we need to move."

The Doctor stepped forward, his expression stern but gentle. "We're not here to play. We're here to find the children and bring them home. Let us pass."

The shadow-children giggled again, the sound sharp and cruel. "Home is here now. They belong to the dark."

Before the Doctor could respond, the figures lunged, dissolving into a mist that wrapped around their legs and pulled them down. Yaz fell to her knees, trying to fight off the suffocating tendrils that crawled up her arms. Emily screamed as the mist clung to her, whispering in her ear.

"Your fear makes us stronger," it said, the voice cold and emotionless.

The Doctor struggled to pull free, the sonic screwdriver buzzing in his hand. He aimed it at the ground, emitting a pulse of bright light that forced the mist to retreat, shrieking as it dissipated.

"Come on, up!" the Doctor urged, pulling Yaz and Emily to their feet. "We need to keep moving. They're trying to separate us, to make us lose hope."

Emily's eyes were wide with terror, tears streaming down her face. "I can hear them, Doctor. They're crying for help. They're close."

The Doctor's face softened, and he nodded. "Then we follow the sound, Emily. Lead the way."

Emily took a shaky breath and pointed to a jagged path that twisted through the dark landscape, lined with spires that seemed to breathe and shift. As they walked, the world around them grew more warped.

The sky pulsed, the ground groaned, and whispers followed them like an ever-present wind.

Yaz glanced at the Doctor, her voice low. "How do we fight something that's everywhere? It's like this place is a part of him."

The Doctor's eyes were shadowed, thoughts racing. "We fight by not giving in to the fear, Yaz. We stay focused. This realm can't exist without a source, and that source is what we need to find."

A sudden, piercing scream echoed through the darkness, freezing them in their tracks. It was the unmistakable cry of a child. Emily's face turned pale, but she set her jaw, moving forward with newfound determination.

They followed the sound to a clearing where a massive, twisted structure loomed—a castle made of shadow and bone. The walls seemed to move, shapes forming and dissolving as if the entire building were alive. The Doctor's eyes narrowed as he surveyed it.

"Inside there," he said. "That's where he's keeping them."

The Boogeyman's voice resonated through the clearing, deep and mocking. "You've come so far, Time Lord. But this is where your hope ends."

The Doctor stood tall, eyes blazing with defiance. "You're wrong. This is where your power ends. You may control the shadows, but you don't control us."

The air grew colder, and the ground beneath them cracked, shadows seeping out and reaching for them like grasping hands. Yaz stepped forward, her voice ringing out. "We're not afraid of you. And we're taking them back."

The Boogeyman's eyes appeared above the castle, twin orbs of crimson fire. "Try, and watch as the darkness consumes you."

The Doctor turned to Yaz and Emily, a fierce resolve in his gaze. "Stay close, no matter what. This ends now."

And with that, they stepped into the castle of shadows, prepared to face the greatest nightmare of all.

Chapter 12: The Boogey Army

The interior of the castle was even more surreal than its exterior. The walls, made of a living substance that shifted between bone and shadow, pulsed with a dark energy that sent shivers through Yaz and Emily. The Doctor's eyes were sharp as he led the way, his sonic screwdriver gripped tightly in one hand.

"We need to find the children and the heart of this place before it overwhelms us," the Doctor said, his voice steady but urgent.

Emily's small voice echoed in the eerie silence. "I can still hear them crying, Doctor. They're scared."

The Doctor nodded, his face set with determination. "Then we don't let them down."

As they moved deeper into the structure, the air grew heavier, pressing against them like an unseen force. Yaz shivered as they turned a corner and found themselves in a vast hall lined with grotesque, shadowy figures. Each one was shaped like a twisted version of the Boogeyman, smaller and more feral, their hollow eyes glowing with a sickly red light.

Yaz sucked in a breath. "Doctor, I think we've found the welcoming committee."

The figures shifted, moving in sync like marionettes controlled by an unseen hand. They stepped forward, their movements jerky and inhuman. The hall filled with a low growl, a sound that resonated with the primal fear in their bones.

The Doctor stepped forward, raising a hand. "I know you can understand me. You don't need to do this. We're not here to fight."

One of the creatures hissed, its voice a chorus of distorted, overlapping tones. "You trespass in his domain. You bring light where only darkness should reign. You will not leave."

The Doctor's eyes narrowed. "I didn't come here to disrupt your world. I came to save the children your master stole. You don't have to serve him."

The creatures' eyes flashed in unison, and they began to close in, their forms rippling with shadow. Yaz glanced at Emily, who clutched her hand with trembling fingers. "Doctor, they're not listening."

The Doctor's jaw clenched as he raised the sonic screwdriver, emitting a high-frequency pulse that sent a wave of light rippling through the hall. The lesser boogeymen shrieked, their forms distorting as they flinched back. But only for a moment.

They regrouped, eyes blazing with fury. One creature lunged, its elongated limbs reaching for Yaz and Emily. Yaz pushed Emily behind her, raising her flashlight and flicking it on. The beam struck the creature, and it shrieked, recoiling as smoke rose from its shadowy skin.

"Light!" Yaz shouted. "They hate the light!"

The Doctor's eyes lit up with realization. "Brilliant, Yaz!" He adjusted the settings on the sonic screwdriver, creating a beam of pure, focused light that swept through the ranks of the creatures, forcing them back.

But the Boogey Army was relentless. For every step they retreated, they surged forward again, their movements synchronized as if controlled by a single mind. The Doctor's expression grew serious as he continued to emit light, but the strain showed in the tightness of his jaw.

One of the creatures lunged, grabbing the Doctor's arm and wrenching it to the side. The sonic screwdriver fell from his grasp, skittering across the floor. A sudden hush fell over the hall as the creatures paused, their eyes shifting to the fallen tool.

The Doctor's eyes widened, and Yaz felt a pang of fear as the creatures looked up with a collective, eerie grin.

"They know it's our best weapon," Yaz whispered, reaching for the flashlight she'd dropped. "Doctor, what do we do now?"

The Doctor's gaze darted around, assessing their options. "We outsmart them. They're tied to fear, Yaz. But we can use that connection against them."

The creatures began to close in again, their movements more confident. The Doctor took a deep breath and raised his voice. "You are more than just fear. You're fragments, splinters of darkness given form. But you're not real. You're shadows, bound by a master who fears the light."

The creatures hesitated, their steps faltering as if the Doctor's words reached a part of them that understood. The hall quivered, the walls shifting with a deep, resonant hum.

Yaz's eyes lit up. "They're connected to him. If they understand that their power is his leash, we might stand a chance."

The Doctor nodded, stepping forward despite the closeness of the shadow-creatures. "You don't have to serve. You don't have to be bound to his will. There's freedom in defying fear."

A creature at the front of the group paused, its form flickering as if caught between solidity and vapor. The others turned their heads, eyes narrowing with uncertainty. The hum in the hall grew louder, the air crackling with an unseen tension.

"Choose!" the Doctor shouted, his voice reverberating through the hall. "Choose freedom over servitude. Choose light over shadow."

For a moment, time seemed to pause. Then, one by one, the lesser boogeymen began to dissolve, their forms unraveling like threads of dark smoke. They dissipated into the air, their whispers fading to silence. The hall grew brighter as the oppressive darkness lifted, and the Doctor bent to pick up his sonic screwdriver.

Yaz let out a breath she hadn't realized she was holding. "Doctor, they're gone. You did it."

The Doctor's face was tight with concentration as he glanced around. "No, Yaz. Not yet. We've only weakened his hold. The Boogeyman himself is still here, and he'll be more furious than ever."

Emily stepped forward, her small voice breaking the silence. "The children. We have to find them before he does."

The Doctor nodded, eyes gleaming with determination. "You're right, Emily. And with the army gone, he's vulnerable. Let's find those children and end this."

They moved forward, deeper into the castle's twisted halls, the echoes of battle still ringing in their ears. The Boogeyman's lair awaited, and with it, the final confrontation that would decide the fate of the children—and the town that had lived in fear for too long.

Chapter 13: The Lost Ones

The corridors of the Boogeyman's castle wound like the twisted roots of an ancient tree, dark and suffocating. The Doctor led Yaz and Emily deeper into the labyrinth, his sonic screwdriver emitting a faint blue glow that illuminated the shifting walls. The air was heavy, thick with a malevolent energy that pressed against their lungs and dulled their senses.

"Doctor, I don't like this," Yaz whispered, her eyes darting to the undulating shadows that seemed to follow them. "It's as if the whole place is alive."

"It is," the Doctor said, voice tight. "This realm isn't just built of darkness; it *is* the Boogeyman. Every corner, every shadow—it's all part of him."

Emily's small hand clutched Yaz's, trembling as she spoke. "I can hear them, Doctor. They're crying. They're so scared."

The Doctor stopped abruptly in front of a massive, iron-bound door. Its surface was etched with twisting runes that seemed to writhe like worms, alive and pulsing with a sickly red glow. A deep, mournful wail seeped through the cracks, chilling them to the bone.

"This is it," the Doctor said, stepping forward. He examined the door, tracing the runes with his fingers. "It's a prison of fear, designed to amplify their worst nightmares. If we open it without breaking the spell, we'll only make things worse."

Yaz's eyes widened, her grip on Emily tightening. "Then how do we break it without feeding him?"

The Doctor's brow furrowed in concentration. "We don't fight fear with force; we counter it with hope, courage, and light. The spell is strong because it's drawing on the children's fear. We need to replace that with something stronger."

Emily looked up at him, eyes wide but resolute. "What do we do, Doctor?"

He met her gaze, a small smile breaking through the worry. "We show them they're not alone. We give them the strength to face their fears and take back control."

The Doctor took out the sonic screwdriver and aimed it at the center of the door. The runes flared brightly, as if resisting, but the Doctor whispered, "You're not the master here, old friend. These children's courage will be your undoing."

With a flick of the screwdriver, the runes dissolved, the door groaning as it creaked open. Inside, the room was vast, far larger than seemed possible. It was filled with pockets of shadows that moved independently, each containing a child trapped in a loop of their worst nightmare.

A boy sat in a corner, eyes wide as he whispered over and over, "They're coming, they're coming," while his hands clawed at invisible terrors. A girl stood motionless, surrounded by shadowy figures that whispered words of mockery and doubt.

Yaz's heart ached as she looked around. "Doctor, how do we reach them?"

The Doctor stepped into the room, voice calm but commanding. "We break the hold by reminding them who they are. Emily, you know these children. They need to hear your voice."

Emily nodded, swallowing her fear as she stepped forward. She took a deep breath and called out, "Robbie! Alice! It's me, Emily! We're here to help you!"

The boy in the corner, Robbie, lifted his head, eyes clouded with terror. He stared at Emily, recognition flickering through the haze. "Emily?" he whispered, his voice cracking.

The Doctor moved to Robbie's side, kneeling down so that their eyes met. "Yes, Robbie. You're not alone anymore. This is just a dream, one you can wake up from. You need to remember who you are and that you're stronger than the fear."

Robbie's eyes darted around, the shadowy figures around him shifting as if aware of the Doctor's presence. They hissed, advancing toward the Doctor, but he raised the sonic screwdriver and emitted a pulse of light. The shadows retreated, their whispers turning to frustrated growls.

"I'm scared," Robbie said, tears streaming down his face.

"I know," the Doctor said softly. "But fear only has power if we let it. You have friends here, Robbie. Emily, Yaz, and I—we're all here. You just have to take that first step."

Robbie took a deep breath, his small hands clenching into fists as he focused on Emily's voice. "You're not alone," she said again, her tone steady, unwavering.

The darkness around Robbie flickered and began to dissolve, the shadowy forms dissipating like mist. He gasped, looking up at the Doctor with eyes full of hope. The Doctor smiled and placed a hand on his shoulder. "Well done, Robbie."

The other children began to stir, eyes widening as they heard Emily's voice. Yaz moved quickly to a girl named Alice, who stood frozen amidst whispering specters. "Alice, listen to me," Yaz said, her voice firm but kind. "These shadows aren't real. You can fight them."

Alice's eyes were glazed, her body trembling as the whispers swirled around her. "They're saying I'm not good enough. That I'll always be alone."

"No," Yaz said, stepping closer. "You're not alone. We're here, and you're strong enough to face them. Don't listen to the lies."

Alice's lip quivered, and she looked at Yaz, the first tear breaking free. The shadowy figures screamed as they faded, unable to hold their power over her any longer.

The Boogeyman's voice thundered through the room, shaking the walls. "You cannot take them from me! Their fear is mine!"

The Doctor's eyes turned cold as he stood, facing the unseen presence. "You've ruled through fear long enough. But fear is nothing compared to the light of hope."

The children gathered around Emily, Yaz, and the Doctor, their faces filled with relief and confusion. The room began to shake as the Boogeyman's anger reverberated through the castle.

"We need to go," Yaz said, looking at the Doctor. "Now."

The Doctor nodded, ushering the children toward the exit. "This world is crumbling. We've broken his power, but it won't let us leave without a fight."

As they ran, the walls of the castle groaned, shadows clawing desperately at them. But the children's voices rose, no longer cries of fear but shouts of defiance. The darkness fell back, weakened, as they burst through the castle doors and into the shifting landscape outside.

The Boogeyman's final roar echoed behind them, filled with rage and defeat. The Doctor turned to look back, eyes fierce. "Your reign is over. The light has won."

They made their way to the TARDIS, the dark world trembling as if on the brink of collapse. Emily looked up at the Doctor, eyes shining with gratitude. "You really did it. You saved us."

The Doctor smiled, his face softening. "No, Emily. *We* did it. Courage isn't the absence of fear; it's facing it and choosing to act anyway."

As the TARDIS doors closed behind them and the ship roared to life, the Boogey World shrank into nothingness on the monitor, a shadow consumed by its own fading power. The children were safe, and the Doctor knew that for now, the darkness had been banished. But the fight against fear was never truly over. It was a battle fought every day, in every heart that dared to hope.

Chapter 14: The Boogeyman's True Form

The TARDIS hummed with a quiet, steady rhythm as it drifted in the inky void between dimensions. Inside, the Doctor moved with the urgency of realization, flipping switches and scrutinizing the console's readings. The children, now safe and sleeping in a corner of the TARDIS, were wrapped in blankets, their faces still marked with the echoes of fear but softening into peace.

Yaz stood nearby, her eyes trained on the Doctor. "You've been staring at those readings for ages, Doctor. What did we just face back there? It wasn't just a creature, was it?"

The Doctor's eyes met hers, a shadow of deep concern darkening his features. "No, Yaz, it wasn't just one creature. That's what's been gnawing at me. The Boogeyman is more than a singular entity. It's a mask worn by something far older and far more dangerous."

Emily, now awake and listening from her spot by Yaz, piped up, her voice small. "You mean... there's more than one?"

The Doctor nodded solemnly. "Yes, Emily. The Boogeyman is just the face of a collective—a hive mind of ancient beings that have thrived on fear for eons. They manipulate reality itself, drawing strength from the fear they instill. Each 'Boogeyman' is tailored to its victim, a perfect blend of nightmares brought to life."

Yaz's eyes widened as she processed his words. "So, when we thought we were fighting *the* Boogeyman, we were really up against all of them?"

The Doctor's expression hardened as he pressed a series of buttons, projecting a holographic image into the air. It displayed shifting, shadowy figures that morphed and twisted into various forms—each one more terrifying than the last. "Exactly. They are called the *Umbraphages*, shadow eaters. They don't just exist in one world or dimension; they spread across realities, feeding off the primal fear that lies at the heart of every sentient being."

Emily shivered and wrapped her blanket tighter. "But why? Why do they do this?"

The Doctor's eyes softened as he looked at her. "Because fear is powerful, Emily. It can cloud the mind, trap people in loops of terror, and make them feel small and alone. The Umbraphages don't just consume fear; they manipulate it, shape it into forms that can dominate and control. They've been doing this since before there was a name for them."

A low, rumbling chuckle filled the TARDIS, reverberating off the walls and sending a chill through everyone. The lights flickered, casting long, jagged shadows that seemed to reach out with grasping fingers. The Doctor's face turned grim as he gripped the console. "They're here."

Yaz's eyes darted around, her pulse quickening. "How is that possible? We left their world behind."

The voice, dark and cold, resonated again, this time taking shape in the middle of the TARDIS. The shadows coalesced into a figure that shifted between forms—first the gaunt, familiar face of the Boogeyman, then other, less definable but equally horrific shapes. The collective voice of the Umbraphages spoke, layered and echoing.

"You think you have defeated us, Time Lord? We are fear itself. We are legion."

The Doctor squared his shoulders, eyes locked onto the shifting figure. "You're wrong. You might be fear, but you're also bound by it. You've hidden behind masks for so long that you've forgotten what true strength looks like."

The shadow figure leaned forward, its eyes blazing with a crimson glow that seared through the dim light. "And you think *hope* is stronger than fear? Hope is fragile. It breaks under the weight of reality."

Emily stood suddenly, surprising both Yaz and the Doctor. Her small, trembling voice was loud in the silence. "Hope isn't fragile. It's what saved us. And it's stronger than you think."

The shadows rippled, almost as if taken aback. The Doctor seized the moment, voice ringing out clear and defiant. "You heard her. You might be ancient, but you're afraid of what you don't control. And you can't control hope or courage."

The figure hissed, its form destabilizing. The TARDIS shuddered as the collective entity's influence pressed against it, but the ship's glow intensified, pushing back with a warmth that seemed to grow from within. The Doctor glanced down at the console, eyes widening as he saw the readings shift. The TARDIS was responding, amplifying the energy of hope within it.

Yaz felt it too—a pulse, a heartbeat that resonated through her chest, filling her with strength. She stepped forward, joining Emily, her voice steady. "We've already faced our worst fears. We've fought, and we've won. You're just shadows pretending to be more."

The Umbraphages' form began to waver, its edges blurring as if it were being pulled apart by an unseen force. "You cannot destroy us," it spat, the voice fracturing into thousands of whispers.

The Doctor's eyes shone with determination. "No, but we can weaken you. And with enough light, shadows don't stand a chance."

He reached out, activating the TARDIS's core defenses. The console glowed brighter, suffusing the room with a radiant light that pulsed with every beat of their collective resolve. The shadows screamed, the sound splitting the air as they were forced to recede, their presence dissolving into thin wisps of smoke that dissipated into the console room.

The light faded, leaving the room in a peaceful silence. The Doctor exhaled, a small smile breaking through the tension. "They're gone. For now."

Yaz turned to him, eyes still wide. "But they'll be back, won't they?"

The Doctor's smile faded as he met her gaze. "They will. Fear is ancient and ever-present. But so is courage. As long as there are people willing to face the darkness, the Umbraphages can never truly win."

Emily, still clutching her blanket, looked up at the Doctor with eyes that were now filled with something new—hope. "We beat them once. We can do it again."

The Doctor nodded, the glint of a promise in his eyes. "Yes, Emily. We can. And we will."

The TARDIS hummed around them, as if agreeing. The battle with the Boogeyman was over, but the war against the Umbraphages—the embodiment of fear itself—was one they would face again. And when they did, they would be ready, armed with the one thing that shadows could never conquer: light.

Chapter 15: The Doctor's Fear

The TARDIS had settled into a tranquil hum, its interior bathed in the familiar, warm glow. The children were safe, finally reunited with their families, and Yaz sat in the console room, replaying the events of their journey in her mind. But the air still felt heavy, as if the shadows that had threatened them lingered in the corners, waiting for their moment.

The Doctor stood by the console, hands braced on the edge, eyes lost in the swirling lights and dials before him. His usual energy had faded, replaced by a rare, almost imperceptible tremor. Yaz noticed and walked over, her brow furrowed with concern.

"Doctor?" she said gently, breaking the silence. "Is everything alright?"

The Doctor didn't respond at first, his eyes distant. Finally, he exhaled, the sound heavy with weariness. "Yaz, do you ever wonder what happens when we lose? When I fail?"

Yaz's heart tightened at the question. The Doctor was the most steadfast, brilliant force she'd ever known. Hearing doubt in his voice sent a chill through her. "But you don't fail, Doctor. You find a way. Always."

The Doctor's eyes met hers, and for the first time, she saw something she'd never expected—fear. Not the adrenaline-fueled fear of battle, but a deep, haunting terror that seemed to strip him of his usual confidence. "I do, Yaz. More than you know."

Before she could respond, the lights in the TARDIS flickered, and a cold wind swept through the room, extinguishing the warmth. The console room darkened, shadows pooling in the corners and stretching across the walls like ink. A familiar, mocking voice echoed around them.

"You are not immune, Time Lord," it whispered, slithering through the air. "Even you have your fears."

The Doctor's face paled as he turned slowly, his eyes wide. "No. Not here."

The shadows deepened, and a figure emerged from the darkness. It wasn't the towering, monstrous form of the Boogeyman, but something subtler, more insidious. It shifted between forms, wearing faces that spoke of loss, regret, and failure—faces the Doctor recognized.

Yaz stepped back instinctively. "Doctor, what is this? Why does it look... different?"

"It's feeding off me," the Doctor said, voice trembling. "This isn't the Boogeyman we fought; it's my fear, given form."

The shadow grinned, eyes glinting with a cruel light. "You've saved so many, yet so many more have been lost. You remember them, don't you, Doctor? Faces that haunt you in the quiet moments. The lives you couldn't save."

The Doctor's hands clenched, the muscles in his jaw tightening. Images flashed in his mind—Gallifrey burning, companions lost to time and fate, the faces of civilizations wiped out despite his best efforts. The guilt he carried, buried under centuries of bravado and hope, surfaced with a vengeance.

Yaz saw the shift, the way the Doctor's confidence crumbled before her eyes. She stepped forward, voice shaking but resolute. "Doctor, don't listen. It's lying. You've done more good than anyone could ever know."

The shadow turned to Yaz, its form warping into a face she didn't recognize but that made the Doctor flinch. "And what of those who've paid the price for his failures? What will happen when it's *you* next, Yaz?"

Yaz's eyes narrowed, anger surging in her chest. "No. This ends now. Doctor, this isn't real. You need to see that. You've always been the one to pull us out of the dark. Let me do that for you this time."

The Doctor's gaze met hers, confusion and pain warring in his eyes. "Yaz, I can't... I can't let go of them. The faces, the names. They remind me of the cost."

Yaz stepped closer, taking his hand. "And that's why you're different. You carry that weight so the rest of us don't have to. You make the impossible choices, and yes, sometimes things don't go as planned. But that's not failure, Doctor. That's being the only one brave enough to try."

The shadow shuddered, its form destabilizing as Yaz's words pierced through the hold it had on the Doctor. The Doctor's eyes cleared, the storm of doubt slowly receding. The realization that he was not alone, that he had someone to remind him of who he was, gave him strength.

"You're right," the Doctor whispered, squeezing Yaz's hand. He turned to face the shadow, his voice steady. "You're right, Yaz."

The shadow hissed, recoiling as if struck. The Doctor stepped forward, determination returning to his posture. "You're just a reflection of the moments that haunt me, but you're not who I am. I'm more than my mistakes, and I don't stand alone."

A light began to glow from within the Doctor, a golden, warm light that pushed back the dark. The shadow thrashed, shrinking as the room brightened, its voice turning from confident to desperate. "You will always fear failure. It's your curse!"

The Doctor's eyes shone with resolve as the shadow faded to nothingness. "Yes, but I'll always choose to fight it, too."

The TARDIS returned to its warm, familiar hum, the shadows dissipating into the air. Yaz let out a breath she didn't realize she'd been holding, her hand still in the Doctor's. He turned to her, eyes full of gratitude.

"Thank you, Yaz," he said softly. "For reminding me."

She smiled, the tension easing from her shoulders. "Anytime, Doctor. You've done it for me more times than I can count."

Emily, who had watched from the sidelines, walked over and looked up at them with wide eyes. "You weren't scared at all, were you?"

The Doctor knelt, a twinkle of his old mischief returning to his eyes. "Oh, I was, Emily. But that's the thing about fear—it's only as powerful as you let it be."

Yaz looked at the Doctor with newfound respect. "So, what now?"

The Doctor stood, his coat sweeping out behind him as he moved back to the console. "Now, we make sure the Umbraphages know that no matter how many times they try to wield fear against us, we'll be ready. And next time, we won't just survive. We'll win."

The TARDIS's engines roared to life, a sound full of promise and hope. They had faced the darkness and come out stronger, and as long as there was light—however small—it would always be enough to fight back the shadows.

Chapter 16: The Doctor's Plan

The TARDIS hummed with a renewed energy, reflecting the Doctor's revitalized determination. Yaz stood at the console, eyes fixed on the Doctor as he paced around, the gears of his mind turning rapidly. Emily sat nearby, watching him with a mixture of admiration and lingering fear.

The Doctor spun around, pointing his sonic screwdriver at the console with a flourish. "Right! We know that the Boogeyman and his ilk—the Umbraphages—draw their power from fear. They feed on it, amplify it, and use it as a tether between their world and ours."

Yaz raised an eyebrow. "And turning fear into hope will weaken that tether?"

The Doctor nodded, a glint of excitement in his eyes. "Exactly. Fear is powerful, but it's unstable. It thrives in darkness and isolation. Hope, on the other hand, is resilient. It spreads, connecting people, binding them together in defiance of whatever threatens them. If we can amplify hope on a large enough scale, we can destabilize the Boogeyman's grip on both dimensions."

Emily shifted nervously. "But how do we do that, Doctor? People are still so scared."

The Doctor's expression softened as he walked over and knelt beside her. "That's true, Emily. But courage isn't the absence of fear—it's choosing to act despite it. We need to remind the people of this town that they're not alone. That they're stronger together than they ever are apart."

Yaz crossed her arms, her mind racing. "So, what's the plan? We can't just march through town telling people to stop being afraid."

The Doctor's face lit up with that familiar, brilliant smile. "Ah, Yaz, we don't tell them. We show them." He stood up and tapped a few buttons on the console. The projection of the town appeared, its buildings outlined in holographic light. "The TARDIS can send a signal—an emotional wave, if you will—using the psychic network embedded in its matrix. This signal will amplify hope, reaching into the hearts of everyone who hears it."

Emily's eyes widened with awe. "You mean, you can make them feel brave?"

The Doctor smiled at her. "Not exactly. We can't make anyone feel anything, but we can remind them of their bravery. We can create a moment where they remember what it's like to stand together, to face their fears with hope instead of despair."

Yaz's face lit up with understanding. "And that hope will weaken the Boogeyman's hold."

"Precisely!" The Doctor beamed, his fingers dancing over the controls. "But there's a catch. The Boogeyman won't just sit back and let us dismantle his power. He'll fight back, try to fill the town with even more fear to counter the signal. We'll need to hold him off long enough for the hope to take root."

Emily stood, a hint of determination breaking through her nervousness. "I want to help."

The Doctor's expression turned serious as he met her gaze. "It's dangerous, Emily. The Boogeyman will sense this plan, and he'll do everything he can to stop it. Are you sure?"

Emily took a deep breath and nodded. "I'm sure. I don't want to be scared anymore. And I don't want anyone else to be scared, either."

The Doctor's eyes glistened with pride. "Braver than most, Emily. Very well, you're part of the team." He turned to Yaz. "Yaz, I need you at the console to monitor the wave. It has to stay balanced—too much, and it could overwhelm them; too little, and it won't work."

Yaz nodded, rolling up her sleeves. "Got it. Let's do this."

The Doctor activated the TARDIS's communications array, and a low, resonant hum filled the room. The holographic projection of the town flickered, showing its streets and homes as the signal began to weave through them like a thread of golden light.

"Now, Emily," the Doctor said, looking at her, "I need you to speak. Tell them what you felt, and what you discovered. Your voice will be the spark that lights this fire."

Emily swallowed, her small hands clenching at her sides, but she nodded. Yaz moved aside to make room for her, placing a gentle hand on her shoulder for support.

The Doctor flipped a switch, and the hum shifted into a subtle, rhythmic pulse that seemed to reach deep into the air around them. He nodded at Emily, eyes warm with encouragement. "When you're ready."

Emily took a deep breath, and then she began to speak, her voice small but steady. "Everyone, it's me, Emily. I know you're scared. I was too. But I learned something... that fear can't win if we don't let it. The Boogeyman isn't as strong as we think he is. He only wins if we believe we're alone. But we're not."

The projection of the town glowed brighter as her words reached out, carried by the TARDIS's psychic wave. The golden threads of light pulsed and spread, connecting one house to another, weaving a net of hope that slowly pushed back the encroaching darkness.

Yaz's eyes widened as she monitored the readings. "It's working, Doctor. The signal is spreading."

But just as the light began to reach the far corners of the projection, a chilling wind swept through the TARDIS. The temperature dropped, and the shadows in the room thickened, coalescing into the now-familiar shape of the Boogeyman. His eyes burned with fury, and his voice resonated with a growl that vibrated through their chests.

"You dare to challenge me here, Time Lord? In my domain?"

The Doctor stepped in front of Emily, sonic screwdriver in hand. "This isn't your domain anymore. The people you've tormented are taking it back, one heartbeat at a time."

The Boogeyman hissed, and the shadows lunged, writhing toward Emily. But Yaz stepped forward, holding up her flashlight, its beam burning bright as she directed it at the advancing dark. The Boogeyman snarled, recoiling.

"Emily, keep talking!" Yaz shouted, her voice strong despite the tremor in her hand.

Emily nodded, tears brimming but unwavering. "We're stronger together. We have to believe that, and not let fear take over."

The light from the town's projection grew, golden threads weaving tighter until the shadowy form of the Boogeyman began to flicker. He roared, the sound filled with a rage that trembled on the edge of desperation.

The Doctor took a step closer, eyes locked on the faltering figure. "This is what you fear most, isn't it? That we'll remember we're stronger than you. That your power is just an illusion built on lies."

With a final, defiant scream, the Boogeyman's form shattered into a thousand fragments of shadow that dissolved into the air. The room brightened, the hum of the TARDIS returning to a calm, steady rhythm. The golden light from the projection held strong, bathing the console room in a warm glow.

Yaz let out a shaky breath and looked at the Doctor, a smile breaking through her exhaustion. "We did it, Doctor. We turned fear into hope."

The Doctor's grin was wide, eyes filled with relief. "Yes, Yaz. And now, the people of this town will know they're not alone. The Boogeyman and the Umbraphages will think twice before trying this again."

Emily looked up at the Doctor, hope and pride lighting her eyes. "We really did it, didn't we?"

The Doctor knelt, meeting her gaze. "Yes, Emily. You did it. You reminded everyone, including me, that hope isn't just a word. It's what keeps the shadows at bay."

As the TARDIS hummed with a renewed energy, the town outside began to heal, the golden threads of hope weaving through it, stronger than ever before. The battle against fear was not over, but the Doctor, Yaz, and Emily had proven that even in the darkest moments, light could be found and shared. And that was enough to make the Boogeyman tremble.

Chapter 17: The Power of Hope

The TARDIS glided down into the heart of the town square, its blue exterior reflecting the golden glow that now emanated from the homes and streets. The Doctor, Yaz, and Emily stood at the threshold, staring out at the frightened but now hopeful faces gathered outside. The townspeople, parents holding children close, elderly neighbors whispering reassurances, all looked up with a mix of curiosity and trepidation as the Doctor stepped forward.

Yaz followed close behind, her voice firm and filled with conviction. "Everyone, listen up! We know you're scared. We've been through the same darkness you have. But we're here to tell you that you don't have to fight it alone."

A murmur swept through the crowd. Faces softened, eyes shifting from shadowed worry to glimmers of trust. Emily stepped forward, her small voice cutting through the chatter. "The Boogeyman only wins if we let him. We have to believe in each other and ourselves. We have to fight with hope."

The Doctor's eyes gleamed with pride as he surveyed the crowd. He raised his sonic screwdriver, sending a pulse of light into the sky. It burst into a thousand tiny stars, raining down softly, like warm snowflakes. "Hope," the Doctor said, his voice strong, resonating with the power of belief. "It's not just a feeling; it's a force. And together, we can use it to push back the shadows."

A hush fell over the square. The golden light the TARDIS had projected started to spread, touching the buildings, seeping into the crevices where darkness had once thrived. But suddenly, a low, guttural growl rumbled through the air, vibrating the cobblestones beneath their feet.

Yaz's eyes darted to the edges of the square, where the shadows thickened, forming a mass that coalesced into the Boogeyman's shape. He was different now—flickering and unstable, his form shifting between monstrous shapes, as if the power that bound him was unraveling. But his eyes still burned crimson, filled with rage.

"You think hope can defeat me?" he snarled, his voice layered with thousands of whispers. "I am fear incarnate. I have existed since the first nightmares were born."

The crowd recoiled, whispers of fear breaking out again. The Doctor stepped forward, his expression hard and unyielding. "You're right. You've been here since the dawn of time. But so have we. So has hope. Every time a person chooses to face you, you lose a little of your power. And today, we're choosing to stand together."

He turned to the crowd, eyes searching their faces. "Listen to me. You've faced the darkness alone, believing it made you weak. But standing here, side by side, you are stronger than any shadow. Reach out to the person next to you. Hold on to them. Share your stories, your fears, and your courage."

A moment of silence passed, and then Emily reached for Yaz's hand, squeezing it tightly. One by one, others followed suit, clasping hands, linking arms, sharing nervous smiles. The Boogeyman let out a roar, surging forward, but his form shuddered, struggling to maintain shape as the light spread through the town square.

A young boy in the crowd called out, his voice small but clear. "I was scared of the dark every night. But not anymore." He looked at Emily and smiled. "Because now I know I'm not alone."

The Boogeyman writhed, eyes narrowing as he lunged toward the boy, but the golden light pulsed in response, forcing him back. He screamed, a sound that cracked through the air like a storm. "You cannot erase fear! It's in your bones, your very breath!"

The Doctor's eyes locked onto the Boogeyman, a calm confidence in his voice. "You're right. Fear will always exist, but so will the courage to face it. You've spent millennia preying on isolation, on the belief that people are powerless. But look around you. You're losing."

Yaz raised her voice, clear and commanding. "We are not just a town of frightened people. We are mothers and fathers, friends and neighbors. We are brave, even when we're scared."

The Boogeyman's form began to disintegrate, dark tendrils dissolving into the air as the golden light of hope pulsed brighter, spreading to every corner of the square and beyond. The crowd's murmurs turned to laughter and cheers, the sound resonating with a power that pushed the last remnants of darkness into oblivion.

Emily stepped forward, looking up at where the Boogeyman had stood moments before. "We won't be afraid of you anymore," she whispered, but her voice carried, strengthened by the hundreds of people around her.

The Doctor turned, a smile breaking across his face as he watched the people embrace, share stories of their fears and triumphs, the light of hope glowing in their eyes. He glanced at Yaz, who was watching the scene with pride and awe.

"It worked," Yaz said, her voice barely above a whisper.

The Doctor nodded, eyes glistening. "It did. Hope isn't just a light. It's a fire, and once it's shared, it grows."

The last echoes of the Boogeyman faded into the air, leaving only the warmth of golden light and the sound of people discovering their strength. The TARDIS doors swung open behind them, and the Doctor looked out over the square one last time.

"Ready for our next adventure?" he asked Yaz, a playful glint returning to his eyes.

Yaz laughed, the sound full and bright. "Always, Doctor. But for now, let's let them celebrate this victory."

Emily turned to the Doctor, a question in her eyes. "Will he ever come back?"

The Doctor knelt down, meeting her gaze. "There will always be shadows, Emily. But now, this town—and you—know how to face them. And that's enough to keep them at bay."

As the TARDIS doors closed and the ship prepared to dematerialize, the Doctor, Yaz, and Emily stood together, the power of hope still warm in their hearts. They knew that while fear would always exist, so too would the courage to fight it, and that would make all the difference.

Chapter 18: The Collapse of the Boogey World

The TARDIS landed with a jarring thud in the center of the Boogey World's crumbling landscape. The once menacing shadows that dominated the realm now twisted in desperation, their forms flickering and dissolving into the void. The ground beneath the Doctor, Yaz, and Emily pulsed like a fading heartbeat, and the sky above was fractured, with streaks of golden light cutting through the oppressive darkness.

The Doctor stepped out of the TARDIS, his eyes scanning the disintegrating realm. He turned to Yaz and Emily, urgency etched into his face. "This world is collapsing faster than I anticipated. We don't have much time."

Yaz followed close behind, her boots sinking slightly into the unstable ground. "What about the remaining children, Doctor? Are they still here?"

The Doctor raised the sonic screwdriver, scanning the chaotic environment as it emitted a high-pitched whir. The device flickered erratically, reflecting the instability of the realm. "Yes, Yaz, they're still here. Scattered, trapped in pockets of fear. But as hope grows in the real world, those pockets are unraveling. If we don't act quickly, this entire place will collapse with them inside."

Emily tugged at the Doctor's sleeve, her voice trembling but determined. "I'll help. I know what it feels like to be trapped here."

The Doctor crouched down to meet her gaze, his expression soft but firm. "You've done enough, Emily. You've been brave beyond words. But this part is dangerous. You and Yaz stay close to the TARDIS. It's the only stable point left in this world."

Emily's eyes filled with tears, but she nodded. "Okay. Just bring them back."

Yaz stepped forward, shaking her head. "Not a chance, Doctor. You're not doing this alone. If this place is falling apart, you'll need someone to watch your back."

The Doctor hesitated, his gaze shifting between the crumbling horizon and Yaz's resolute expression. Finally, he relented with a sigh. "Fine. But stay close, and if I say run, you run. No arguments."

Yaz smirked. "When do I ever argue?"

The Doctor shot her a knowing look before turning back to the landscape. He pointed toward a cluster of jagged spires that flickered like broken holograms. "The children are over there. Let's move."

As they made their way through the collapsing terrain, the air grew heavier, filled with the sound of distant cries and the occasional roar of collapsing structures. The ground beneath their feet shifted unpredictably, forcing them to move carefully but quickly.

Yaz caught sight of a small figure huddled near the base of one of the spires. "Doctor! Over there!"

They sprinted toward the child, a boy no older than eight, his face pale and streaked with tears. He was surrounded by tendrils of shadow, writhing and grasping at his small frame. The Doctor activated the sonic screwdriver, emitting a pulse of golden light that severed the tendrils and sent them retreating into the void.

The boy looked up, his eyes wide with terror. "Who... who are you?"

The Doctor knelt down, his voice gentle and reassuring. "I'm the Doctor, and I'm here to take you home. Can you walk?"

The boy nodded shakily and took the Doctor's hand. Yaz knelt beside him, her tone soft. "You're safe now. Just stick with us, okay?"

As they continued, more children appeared, each trapped in their own nightmarish scenarios. Some were tangled in webs of shadow, others surrounded by flickering illusions of their worst fears. Each time, the Doctor and Yaz worked together to free them, guiding them back toward the safety of the TARDIS.

But the world around them grew more chaotic with every moment. The spires crumbled, falling into endless chasms that opened like mouths beneath their feet. The sky splintered further, golden light pouring in and dissolving the darkness.

Yaz turned to the Doctor, panic creeping into her voice. "Doctor, this place is falling apart. How much time do we have?"

The Doctor glanced at the horizon, where the boundaries of the Boogey World were collapsing inward like a tidal wave of destruction. "Not enough. We have to move faster."

A roar echoed through the realm, and the shadows began to converge, coalescing into the towering form of the Boogeyman. Though weakened and flickering, his crimson eyes still burned with rage.

"You will not take them!" he bellowed, his voice shaking the ground. "This is my domain, my power. You will all fall with it!"

The Doctor turned, his face hardening. "You're wrong. This isn't your domain anymore. The light is breaking through, and your grip is gone."

The Boogeyman roared again, his shadowy form lashing out. Yaz pulled the children back, shielding them as the Doctor stepped forward, his sonic screwdriver blazing with golden light.

"Your time is over," the Doctor said, his voice rising above the chaos. "Fear may linger, but it no longer rules. Hope has taken root, and you can't stop it."

The Boogeyman lunged, but his form splintered, pieces of shadow breaking away and dissolving into the golden light. With a final, anguished scream, his form collapsed entirely, leaving only a faint echo of his voice. "This is not the end..."

The Doctor turned back to Yaz and the children, his face urgent. "Run! Now!"

They sprinted toward the TARDIS, the ground breaking apart beneath their feet. Yaz carried one of the smaller children, while the Doctor guided the others. The golden light pouring into the realm grew brighter, engulfing the landscape and dissolving the last remnants of shadow.

They reached the TARDIS just as the final collapse began. The Doctor ushered everyone inside, slamming the doors shut behind them. He darted to the console, flipping switches and pulling levers with practiced urgency.

"Hold on, everyone!" he shouted as the TARDIS groaned, shaking violently as it tore free of the collapsing Boogey World.

With a deafening roar, the TARDIS burst through the rift, landing back in the real world with a jarring crash. The children huddled together, their faces pale but relieved. Yaz leaned against the railing, catching her breath.

The Doctor stood at the console, his hands resting on the edge as he looked at the group with a small, tired smile. "We did it. Everyone's safe."

Emily ran to the Doctor, throwing her arms around him. "You saved them!"

The Doctor knelt, hugging her tightly. "No, Emily. *We* saved them. Together."

As the TARDIS doors opened to reveal the bright, welcoming town square, the children stepped out into the waiting arms of their families. The golden light lingered in the air, a reminder that hope had triumphed over fear.

Yaz stood beside the Doctor, watching the joyful reunions with a smile. "You did it again, Doctor."

He glanced at her, his grin wide and full of pride. "No, Yaz. *We* did. Fear may be ancient, but hope is eternal. And today, we proved that."

Chapter 19: The Final Showdown

The TARDIS had barely settled back into the town square when a low, guttural growl echoed through the air. The joyous reunions paused as an unnatural chill swept over the crowd. Shadows began pooling around the edges of the square, stretching and coiling like living things. The townsfolk huddled together, eyes wide with dread as the ground trembled beneath their feet.

The Doctor stepped out of the TARDIS, sonic screwdriver in hand, his face a mask of steely determination. Yaz followed, her flashlight raised, while Emily stood close, her small hands balled into fists. Above them, the golden light that had pierced the Boogey World began to dim, overtaken by a creeping, suffocating darkness.

And then he appeared.

The Boogeyman emerged from the shadows, his once-towering form now flickering and unstable. His edges frayed like smoke in a strong wind, but his crimson eyes burned brighter than ever, filled with rage and desperation.

"You dare to think you've defeated me?" the Boogeyman snarled, his voice fractured and layered with countless whispers. "You've only delayed the inevitable."

The Doctor took a step forward, his expression calm but unyielding. "You're right about one thing—you're inevitable. Fear will always exist. But so will hope. And as long as there's hope, you'll never win."

The Boogeyman's grin widened, jagged and menacing. "Hope? Hope is fragile. It shatters under the weight of reality. I have existed for eons, feeding on the fear that lies at the core of every living being. You are nothing but a momentary flicker in the vast darkness."

The Doctor's eyes glinted with defiance. "And yet, that flicker is enough to send you trembling."

The Boogeyman lunged, his shadowy form sweeping toward the Doctor like a tidal wave. The Doctor raised the sonic screwdriver, emitting a brilliant burst of golden light that struck the creature, forcing him back with a howl of fury.

"Not this time," the Doctor said, his voice ringing with authority. "You've ruled through fear for too long, but you've forgotten the one thing that always brings fear to its knees."

The Boogeyman hissed, his form shuddering. "And what is that, Time Lord?"

"Knowledge," the Doctor said, stepping closer. "You thrive in the shadows because you think no one can understand you. But I see you for what you are—a parasite. A collective of shadows clinging to the fear of others to survive."

The creature recoiled, his form wavering. "I am more than that! I am the dark that consumes all light!"

The Doctor's smile was grim. "No, you're just a shadow afraid of being forgotten. And that's exactly what's happening."

He turned to the townsfolk, his voice rising. "Everyone, listen to me! This isn't a monster. It's just a collection of fears given form. It has no power unless we let it."

The Boogeyman roared, his voice shaking the air. "Do not listen to him! I am your nightmares! I am the reason you shiver in the dark!"

Emily stepped forward, her small voice cutting through the noise. "You're nothing. You tried to scare us, but we're not scared anymore. We have each other."

The townsfolk began to murmur, their fear giving way to courage as they took Emily's words to heart. One by one, they stepped forward, standing together in defiance of the Boogeyman.

The shadows around the creature began to fray, unraveling like threads pulled from a tapestry. The golden light from the TARDIS grew brighter, pushing back the darkness as hope surged through the crowd.

The Boogeyman screamed, his form flickering violently. "You think this changes anything? Fear will always return! I am eternal!"

The Doctor's voice was quiet but resolute. "Maybe fear will return. But so will we. Every time."

He raised the sonic screwdriver, its light merging with the golden glow of the TARDIS. The combined radiance engulfed the Boogeyman, his form disintegrating piece by piece. As he dissolved, his voice turned from a roar to a desperate whisper.

"You cannot destroy me... I will always... be..."

And then, he was gone. The shadows dissipated, leaving only the warm glow of the golden light that bathed the town square. The ground beneath them stilled, and a deep, collective breath of relief swept through the crowd.

The Doctor lowered the sonic screwdriver, his shoulders relaxing for the first time in what felt like hours. Yaz let out a shaky laugh, lowering her flashlight. "Is it over?"

The Doctor turned to her, a small, weary smile on his face. "For now. Fear never truly disappears, Yaz. But neither does hope. And as long as we hold onto that, we'll always have the upper hand."

Emily ran up to him, her face glowing with pride. "You did it, Doctor! You stopped him!"

The Doctor knelt down, placing a hand on her shoulder. "No, Emily. *We* stopped him. It was your courage—and everyone's—that made the difference."

The townsfolk began to cheer, their voices ringing out in celebration. Parents hugged their children, neighbors embraced, and the air was filled with the warmth of triumph. The Doctor stood, watching with a quiet satisfaction as hope reclaimed the hearts of the people.

Yaz nudged him gently. "What's next, Doctor?"

He turned to her, his grin widening. "Oh, Yaz. There's always another adventure waiting, another shadow to confront. But for now, I think we've earned a moment to enjoy the light."

As the TARDIS hummed in agreement, the Doctor, Yaz, and Emily stood together, watching as the town basked in the power of hope—a force stronger than any fear, and a reminder that even in the darkest moments, light would always find a way.

Chapter 20: The Return Home

The TARDIS materialized in the heart of the town square with its usual wheezing groan, but this time, it brought a wave of warmth and relief. The children, weary but safe, stood behind the Doctor, Yaz, and Emily, their wide eyes reflecting the light of the dawn breaking over the town. The golden rays pierced through the lingering mist, chasing away the last remnants of the Boogeyman's shadow.

Parents rushed forward, tears streaming down their faces as they embraced their children. The square filled with cries of joy, laughter, and the murmur of gratitude. Emily watched the reunions, her small face glowing with pride.

Yaz turned to the Doctor, a smile breaking through her exhaustion. "Well, that's one nightmare we won't be revisiting anytime soon."

The Doctor chuckled softly, leaning on the TARDIS console as if finally allowing himself a moment to breathe. "Let's hope not. But nightmares have a funny way of creeping back in, don't they?"

Yaz raised an eyebrow. "Always the optimist."

The Doctor's smile faded slightly, his eyes scanning the horizon. "It's not about optimism, Yaz. It's about being prepared. Fear will always exist—it's as much a part of life as hope. But it doesn't have to rule us."

Emily stepped forward, her small voice breaking into their conversation. "Doctor, do you think he's really gone? The Boogeyman?"

The Doctor knelt down to her level, his gaze steady and reassuring. "Gone? For now, yes. But fear, Emily... fear is never truly gone. It's part of being alive. But you've learned the most important lesson: fear can only control you if you let it. And you—you've proven you're stronger than that."

Emily smiled, her confidence shining through. "And if he ever comes back?"

The Doctor's grin widened. "Then you'll know exactly how to beat him. And if you ever need help, you've got a friend in a blue box."

As the square began to settle, the Doctor and Yaz walked among the townsfolk, listening to their stories of fear and survival. Mr. Johnson, Emily's father, approached them, his face a mixture of gratitude and lingering concern.

"Doctor, I don't know how to thank you," he said, his voice thick with emotion. "You brought them back. You gave us hope."

The Doctor placed a hand on Mr. Johnson's shoulder. "You don't need to thank me. Your daughter did most of the hard work. Hope wasn't mine to give—it was already here, waiting to be found."

Mr. Johnson's gaze shifted to Emily, who was now surrounded by other children, her laughter carrying on the breeze. "She's changed. Stronger. Braver."

Yaz smiled, folding her arms. "She's a hero. You should be proud."

The Doctor's face turned thoughtful as he looked at the children. "The real healing starts now. The Boogeyman may be gone, but the memories of fear linger. It's up to all of you to remind each other that no matter how dark it gets, the light is always there."

Later, as the sun climbed higher, the Doctor stood by the TARDIS, watching the town slowly come back to life. Emily approached, her small hand clutching a folded piece of paper.

"I made this for you," she said shyly, holding it out to him.

The Doctor took the paper, unfolding it to reveal a child's drawing. It depicted the TARDIS surrounded by golden light, with stick figures of the Doctor, Yaz, and Emily standing together. At the bottom, in uneven handwriting, were the words *Thank you for saving us.*

The Doctor's expression softened as he looked at the drawing, his voice quiet. "This... this is brilliant, Emily. Absolutely brilliant."

Yaz leaned over to look and grinned. "We make a pretty good team, don't we?"

Emily beamed. "The best."

As the Doctor and Yaz prepared to leave, the townsfolk gathered around the TARDIS, their faces filled with gratitude and hope. Emily stood at the front, waving enthusiastically.

"Will we ever see you again?" she called out.

The Doctor paused at the door, turning to face the crowd. "Who knows? The universe has a funny way of bringing people back together. But remember this—whenever fear tries to take hold, look to each other. Hope is always stronger when it's shared."

With a final wave, the Doctor stepped inside the TARDIS, Yaz close behind. The door closed, and the familiar sound of the engines began to echo through the square.

Inside, Yaz leaned against the console, watching as the Doctor fiddled with the controls. "You know, you could've stayed a bit longer. They adore you."

The Doctor's hands paused, his eyes distant. "It's not about being adored, Yaz. It's about letting them find their own strength. They don't need me anymore."

Yaz tilted her head, studying him. "But we all need a reminder now and then, don't we?"

The Doctor's lips curved into a small, knowing smile. "Yes, Yaz. That's why I have you."

The TARDIS dematerialized, leaving the town behind as it journeyed to its next destination. And while the Doctor and Yaz moved forward, the small town—once ruled by fear—stood strong, bathed in the light of hope that would carry it through any darkness.

Chapter 21: Loose Ends

The TARDIS hummed softly in the middle of the town square, its blue exterior a comforting beacon of hope amidst the rebuilding effort. The once-shadowed town was alive with activity, parents mending broken homes, children running and laughing, and neighbors working together to erase the scars of fear. The golden light that had spread during the final confrontation lingered in the air, giving everything a soft, warm glow.

The Doctor leaned against the TARDIS door, watching with a quiet smile as the townsfolk reclaimed their lives. Yaz approached, her boots crunching on the cobblestones. She carried two steaming cups of tea, handing one to the Doctor.

"Thought you might need this," Yaz said, nodding toward the horizon. "You've been standing there for ages."

The Doctor took the cup with a grateful smile. "Thanks, Yaz. Just making sure the seals are holding."

Yaz frowned, looking around. "The seals? I thought we shut the Boogey World for good."

The Doctor sipped his tea, his expression turning serious. "We did. But dimensions like that don't just vanish. They shift, looking for weak spots to latch onto. I'm making sure there's no way for it to reconnect to this town—or anywhere else."

Yaz sighed, running a hand through her hair. "And if it does?"

The Doctor's eyes gleamed with a mix of determination and caution. "Then we stop it. Again."

As the day wore on, the Doctor moved through the town, checking his sonic screwdriver against invisible traces of residual energy. He paused outside Emily's house, scanning the area as Yaz followed close behind.

"Still something here?" Yaz asked, watching the Doctor wave the screwdriver over the ground.

"Residual rift energy," the Doctor replied. "Nothing dangerous, but it's like a scar on reality. It'll fade with time, but I want to make sure there's no chance of it reopening."

As he worked, the door to the house creaked open, and Emily stepped out. She clutched her favorite stuffed animal, a slightly worn bunny with floppy ears, and hesitated before approaching.

"Doctor?" she called, her small voice tentative but steady.

The Doctor turned, his face lighting up. "Emily! Everything alright?"

Emily nodded, her expression serious. "I just... I wanted to thank you. For saving me and my friends. For saving everyone."

The Doctor crouched down, meeting her eyes. "No thanks necessary, Emily. You were the real hero. You showed everyone that courage isn't about not being scared—it's about facing the fear and standing tall anyway."

Emily blushed, hugging her bunny tighter. "But I still have a question."

Yaz tilted her head. "What is it, Emily?"

The little girl hesitated, her eyes flicking between Yaz and the Doctor. "Will the Boogeyman ever come back?"

The Doctor's expression softened, and he reached out to place a hand on Emily's shoulder. "Fear, Emily, is like a shadow. It'll always be there, lurking at the edges. But that doesn't mean it has to rule us. The Boogeyman and his kind might try to find another way, but now you—and everyone in this town—know how to fight back. You've beaten him once. You can do it again."

Emily's eyes glistened, her small face set with determination. "But what if we can't? What if he gets stronger?"

The Doctor gave her a warm smile, his voice gentle. "If that ever happens, and it feels like the shadows are too big to face alone, you remember this: you're never alone. You've got your family, your friends, and—" he gestured to the TARDIS behind him "—a certain blue box that's always ready to help."

Emily nodded slowly, her confidence growing. "I'll remember."

The Doctor stood, brushing off his coat. "Good. Now, off you go. You've got a world to explore, and it's much brighter than it was yesterday."

Emily grinned and dashed back inside, her laughter echoing behind her. Yaz watched her go, a small smile on her lips.

"She's going to be okay," Yaz said softly.

The Doctor nodded, slipping his hands into his pockets. "She's stronger than she knows. They all are."

Later that evening, as the sun dipped below the horizon, the Doctor and Yaz gathered in the TARDIS for one final check. The console glowed warmly as the Doctor reviewed the energy readings. Satisfied, he leaned back, exhaling a long breath.

"All loose ends tied up," he declared. "The Boogey World is sealed, the rift energy is fading, and this town is back on its feet."

Yaz leaned against the console, watching him. "You don't seem as relieved as I thought you'd be."

The Doctor gave her a wry smile. "Relieved, yes. But there's always the next challenge, Yaz. The next shadow to confront. It never truly ends."

Yaz nodded, her voice thoughtful. "But that's why you keep going, isn't it? Because even if the shadows never end, neither does the light."

The Doctor looked at her, a glimmer of pride in his eyes. "Exactly. Well said, Yaz."

She grinned, straightening. "So, where to next?"

The Doctor tapped a few buttons on the console, the TARDIS groaning as it prepared to dematerialize. "Anywhere the shadows are too dark and the light needs a little help."

With a final flick of a lever, the TARDIS disappeared from the quiet town, leaving behind only the faint echo of its engines. And in the town square, where the blue box had stood, the golden light of hope remained, a lasting reminder that even in the face of fear, the courage to stand together could illuminate the darkest corners.

Chapter 22: The Doctor's Farewell

The golden hues of dawn crept across the town square, softening the edges of the cobblestone streets and illuminating the smiles of the townsfolk as they worked together to rebuild. The TARDIS stood in its usual commanding presence, though it felt less like a mysterious oddity and more like a part of the town—a comforting reminder of the light that had triumphed over the shadows.

The Doctor leaned against the blue doors, watching the scene unfold with quiet satisfaction. Yaz stood beside him, hands on her hips, a knowing smile playing on her lips.

"You've done it again, Doctor," she said. "Saved the day, made some friends, and left a town stronger than ever."

The Doctor tilted his head, a small grin breaking through. "Not bad for a few days' work, eh?"

Before Yaz could respond, the familiar sound of small footsteps reached their ears. Emily came running up to them, her stuffed bunny clutched tightly in one hand. Her eyes sparkled with gratitude and sadness as she stopped in front of the Doctor.

"Are you leaving?" she asked, her voice small but steady.

The Doctor crouched down, meeting her gaze. "Yes, Emily. It's time for Yaz and me to move on. There's a big universe out there, and someone's got to keep it in check."

Emily's bottom lip trembled. "But... what if the Boogeyman comes back? What if we need you?"

The Doctor reached into his coat pocket, pulling out a small, intricate device. It was no larger than a pocket watch, with a shimmering surface that seemed to catch the light in impossible ways. Its center glowed faintly, a warm, golden hue.

"This," the Doctor said, holding it out to her, "is something very special. I call it a Beacon. If you're ever in trouble—if the Boogeyman or anything else comes back—all you have to do is press this button here." He pointed to the glowing center. "It'll send a signal directly to me, no matter where I am."

Emily's eyes widened as she reached out to take the device, cradling it in her hands like a priceless treasure. "Really? You'll come back?"

The Doctor smiled softly, his voice gentle. "Of course I will. But remember, Emily, you're stronger than you think. You've already beaten the Boogeyman once, and you've shown everyone here how to stand up to fear. That's a power that can't be taken away."

Emily nodded, her grip tightening on the Beacon. "I'll take care of it. I promise."

Yaz knelt beside her, ruffling her hair. "We know you will, Emily. You're a little hero now."

Emily grinned, her sadness giving way to pride. "I'll make sure everyone remembers what you taught us."

As the Doctor stood to his full height, the townsfolk began to gather around the TARDIS, their expressions a mix of gratitude and sorrow. Mr. Johnson stepped forward, Emily's father, his voice thick with emotion.

"Doctor, Yaz... we don't know how to thank you for everything you've done. You've given us back our children, our lives."

The Doctor waved him off with a good-natured smile. "No need for thanks. Just keep looking after each other. That's all the thanks I need."

Mr. Johnson nodded, his hand resting on Emily's shoulder. "We will. And if the Boogeyman ever tries to come back—"

"He won't stand a chance," the Doctor finished, his tone light but firm.

The time came for goodbyes. Emily stepped forward one last time, her Beacon held tightly in her hand. "Will you tell me one thing before you go, Doctor?"

The Doctor tilted his head, curious. "What's that, Emily?"

She hesitated, her brow furrowing in thought. "Why do you keep doing it? Saving people like us? You don't have to, but you do anyway. Why?"

The Doctor's face softened, and for a moment, a flicker of something ancient and wistful crossed his features. "Because someone once showed me that even in the darkest corners of the universe, there's always a reason to hope. A reason to fight for the light. And every time I see someone like you, Emily—someone brave enough to stand up and say 'no' to the shadows—it reminds me why I keep going."

Emily beamed, her heart swelling with pride. "I'll remember that."

The Doctor stepped back, giving her a mock salute. "See that you do. And remember, one push of that button, and I'll be here faster than you can say 'TARDIS.'"

Yaz placed a hand on the TARDIS door, glancing back at the crowd. "Take care of yourselves, yeah? And don't forget—you've got this."

The townsfolk waved as the Doctor and Yaz disappeared into the TARDIS. The door closed, and the sound of the engines filled the air, a rhythmic wheezing that sent a comforting vibration through the ground.

Inside the TARDIS, Yaz leaned against the console, watching as the Doctor adjusted the settings. "That Beacon—does it really work anywhere?"

The Doctor grinned, a mischievous glint in his eye. "Oh, absolutely. If Emily ever needs me, the TARDIS will find her."

Yaz smirked, crossing her arms. "You really care about that kid, don't you?"

The Doctor's hands stilled for a moment, and he looked up, his expression soft. "She's the kind of hope this universe needs more of, Yaz. Someone who doesn't just fight fear but teaches others how to do the same. How could I not?"

Yaz nodded, her respect for the Doctor deepening. "So, where to next?"

The Doctor flipped a lever, the TARDIS lurching into motion. "Anywhere the shadows gather, Yaz. There's always work to be done."

As the TARDIS soared through the vortex, Emily stood in the town square, the Beacon glowing faintly in her hands. She watched the golden light fade from the sky, her heart full of gratitude and courage. She knew the Doctor was right—fear would always exist. But so would the light to face it, and now, she carried a piece of that light with her, ready to shine whenever the shadows returned.

Chapter 23: A New Beginning

The town was bathed in the soft, golden glow of a new morning. The square, once filled with terrified whispers and shadowy threats, now buzzed with the sound of hammers, laughter, and chatter. Parents worked together to mend broken fences, repair shattered windows, and paint over the scars left by the Boogeyman's reign. Children, once too afraid to leave their homes, played freely, their laughter echoing through the air.

Emily stood with a group of her friends near the fountain in the center of the square. They huddled around her as she proudly showed off the Beacon the Doctor had given her. The small device shimmered faintly in the sunlight, drawing awe and curiosity from her peers.

"Do you think he'll really come back if you press it?" Robbie asked, his voice full of wonder.

Emily grinned, clutching the Beacon tightly. "Of course he will. The Doctor always keeps his promises."

Alice, one of the older children, crossed her arms and gave Emily a teasing smile. "You're pretty lucky. I mean, who else can say they've got a friend like the Doctor?"

Emily nodded, her expression growing thoughtful. "We all do. He didn't just save me—he saved all of us."

Yaz leaned against the TARDIS, watching the scene with a soft smile. "Look at them. Just a few days ago, they were too scared to even come outside. Now they're running around like nothing happened."

The Doctor stood beside her, his hands in his coat pockets. His eyes were fixed on the children, a mixture of pride and contemplation in his gaze. "Resilience, Yaz. Humans have it in spades. It's what makes you lot so brilliant."

Yaz chuckled, nudging him with her elbow. "Coming from you, I'll take that as a compliment."

The Doctor didn't respond immediately, his expression growing more serious. "Fear can be a heavy thing. It clings, lingers in the quiet corners of the mind. But the beauty of humans is that you don't let it define you. You learn, you adapt, and you grow."

Yaz tilted her head, studying him. "You sound like someone who knows fear pretty well."

The Doctor's lips twitched into a wry smile. "Oh, Yaz. I've danced with fear more times than I can count. Fear of losing people, fear of failing, fear of not being enough. But you know what I've learned?"

Yaz raised an eyebrow. "What?"

"That fear's just a reminder," the Doctor said softly, his voice steady. "A reminder that something matters. That there's something worth fighting for."

Yaz's smile widened, her respect for him deepening. "That's a pretty good way to look at it."

The Doctor nodded, his gaze shifting back to the children. "They'll remember this, Yaz. Maybe not every detail, but they'll remember that they faced the dark and won. That's the kind of memory that shapes people."

Across the square, Mr. Johnson approached Emily, who was now busy organizing an impromptu game with the other children. He knelt beside her, his expression a mix of gratitude and fatherly pride.

"Emily," he said gently, "I just wanted to say how proud I am of you. You were so brave, even when everything felt so scary."

Emily looked up at him, her eyes bright. "I had to be, Dad. The Doctor said fear only wins if we let it."

Mr. Johnson smiled, ruffling her hair. "Sounds like the Doctor taught you some pretty important lessons."

Emily nodded, clutching her stuffed bunny and the Beacon. "He said I'm stronger than I think. And he's right."

As the day wore on and the town's repairs continued, the Doctor and Yaz began to make their rounds. They checked in with families, offering kind words and gentle reassurances. The Doctor even joined the children for a short game of tag, his laughter mingling with theirs as he darted between the cobblestone streets with surprising agility.

When the sun began to dip below the horizon, painting the sky in hues of orange and pink, the Doctor and Yaz returned to the TARDIS. The townsfolk gathered to bid them farewell, their faces glowing with gratitude.

"Doctor, Yaz," Mr. Johnson called out, stepping forward. "You didn't just save this town—you gave us hope. I don't think we can ever repay you."

The Doctor waved him off with a grin. "Oh, don't be silly. You've already repaid me by proving that hope is stronger than fear. That's worth more than all the thanks in the universe."

Emily ran up to them one last time, the Beacon clutched tightly in her hand. "Doctor, Yaz, will you ever come back?"

The Doctor crouched down, meeting her gaze with a gentle smile. "The universe is a big place, Emily. I've got a lot of corners to check and shadows to chase. But if you ever need me, you know how to call."

Emily nodded, her face solemn but determined. "I won't forget."

Yaz knelt beside her, ruffling her hair one last time. "And don't forget what you've learned, either. You've got a town full of people looking up to you now. Don't let them down."

Emily beamed, her confidence shining through. "I won't."

As the TARDIS dematerialized, its familiar wheezing echoing through the square, the townsfolk waved, their cheers of gratitude filling the air. Emily stood at the front, holding the Beacon close to her heart as the blue box disappeared into the stars.

Inside the TARDIS, Yaz leaned against the console, watching the Doctor as he set their next course. "So, where to now?"

The Doctor grinned, his hands flying over the controls. "Oh, Yaz, you know me. Wherever there's a shadow too dark or a fear too strong, that's where we'll be."

Yaz laughed, shaking her head. "And here I thought we might get a quiet day."

The Doctor's grin widened. "Not a chance."

As the TARDIS sped through the time vortex, the town below began a new chapter, its people stronger, braver, and more united than ever. And though the Boogeyman's shadow was gone, the light of hope the Doctor had left behind ensured that they would never be powerless against fear again.

Chapter 24: The Shadow Lurks

The TARDIS hurtled through the time vortex, its interior humming with a familiar rhythm that spoke of stability and power. Yaz leaned against the console, sipping a mug of tea the Doctor had hastily brewed. The golden light of the time rotor bathed the room in a soft glow, but something about the air felt heavier than usual.

The Doctor stood by the console, one hand on a lever, the other gripping his sonic screwdriver. His face, which had been alight with triumph and satisfaction just moments ago, was now marked by a faint frown.

Yaz noticed the change immediately. "Alright, what's going on? You've got that 'something's wrong but I'm not telling anyone yet' look."

The Doctor glanced at her, his usual playful energy dimmed. "What makes you think something's wrong, Yaz?"

She raised an eyebrow, crossing her arms. "Oh, I don't know. Maybe the fact that you're gripping that lever like it's the only thing keeping the TARDIS together."

The Doctor blinked, then loosened his grip, forcing a sheepish smile. "Caught me, have you?"

Yaz stepped closer, her voice softer now. "Doctor, what is it? I thought we beat the Boogeyman."

The Doctor turned to the monitor, scanning the swirling patterns of the vortex. His brow furrowed deeper as he studied the readings. "We did. At least, I think we did. But there's... something."

Yaz leaned over his shoulder, squinting at the screen. "Something like what?"

The Doctor tapped the monitor, his voice low and cautious. "A disturbance. Subtle, almost imperceptible, but it's there. A ripple in the fabric of reality, like a crack trying to form."

Yaz frowned. "You think it's the Boogeyman?"

The Doctor straightened, running a hand through his hair. "I don't know. It doesn't feel like him, but it's... familiar. Like the echo of a shadow that shouldn't be there."

The TARDIS suddenly jolted, the lights flickering as the hum of the engines grew uneven. Yaz grabbed onto the console, her tea spilling across the floor. "Doctor, what's happening?"

The Doctor's hands flew over the controls, flipping switches and pulling levers as the TARDIS groaned in protest. "Something's pulling at us. A gravitational anomaly, but it's not natural. It's... deliberate."

Yaz's eyes widened. "Deliberate? You mean someone—or something—is doing this?"

The Doctor nodded, his face grim. "Exactly. And whatever it is, it wants us to stop."

The TARDIS shook violently again, and the lights dimmed, casting the room into shadow. The Doctor steadied himself, his voice rising above the chaos. "Hold on, Yaz. We're going to see what this thing wants."

With a final pull of the main lever, the TARDIS came to an abrupt halt. The engines groaned one last time before falling silent, leaving the console room bathed in an eerie stillness. The Doctor and Yaz exchanged a look before the Doctor moved to the door.

"Stay behind me," he said, his tone leaving no room for argument.

Yaz grabbed her flashlight from the console and followed him. "You know I'm not staying behind."

The Doctor rolled his eyes but didn't argue further. He pushed open the TARDIS doors, revealing a dark and lifeless landscape. The ground was cracked and barren, stretching out into a horizon shrouded in mist. The air was cold, carrying a faint, metallic tang that made Yaz shiver.

"Where are we?" Yaz asked, her voice hushed.

The Doctor scanned the area with his sonic screwdriver, his frown deepening. "A pocket dimension. Newly formed, by the looks of it. It's unstable, which means someone—or something—created it recently."

A low, guttural sound echoed through the mist, sending a chill down their spines. Yaz tightened her grip on the flashlight, her eyes darting around. "Doctor, I don't think we're alone."

The Doctor nodded, his expression grim. "Neither do I."

They moved cautiously through the desolate terrain, the mist swirling around them like living tendrils. The sound grew louder, a rhythmic pulse that seemed to come from all directions at once. Yaz glanced at the Doctor, her nerves fraying. "What's making that noise?"

The Doctor didn't answer immediately. He was focused on the sonic screwdriver, which emitted a faint, erratic whine. Finally, he stopped, his face pale. "It's not a noise, Yaz. It's a heartbeat."

Yaz's breath hitched. "A heartbeat? Of what?"

The Doctor turned to her, his eyes shadowed with worry. "Of this dimension. It's alive."

Before Yaz could respond, the mist parted, revealing a figure standing in the distance. It was humanoid in shape, but its edges were blurred, as if it were made of smoke and shadow. Its eyes glowed faintly, a dull red that sent a shiver down Yaz's spine.

The Doctor stepped forward, his voice steady but wary. "Who are you? What do you want?"

The figure didn't move, but its voice echoed through the air, deep and layered. "You meddle where you should not, Time Lord. You think you have banished fear, but fear cannot be destroyed. It waits, it watches, and it grows."

Yaz felt a chill run down her spine. "Doctor... is that him? Is it the Boogeyman?"

The Doctor's jaw tightened as he studied the figure. "No. It's something else. Something older."

The figure's voice grew louder, resonating in their bones. "You may have sealed one door, but countless others remain. You cannot protect them all."

The Doctor squared his shoulders, his voice ringing with defiance. "Maybe not. But I can protect this one. And if you think you can scare me into giving up, you've picked the wrong Time Lord."

The figure tilted its head, its red eyes narrowing. "We shall see."

Before they could react, the ground beneath them cracked, and a wave of shadow surged forward, engulfing the landscape. The Doctor grabbed Yaz's hand, pulling her back toward the TARDIS as the shadow closed in.

"Run!" he shouted, his voice cutting through the chaos.

They sprinted toward the TARDIS, the shadow nipping at their heels. Yaz stumbled, but the Doctor caught her, pulling her through the doors just as the shadow slammed against the exterior. The TARDIS shuddered but held firm.

Inside, the Doctor raced to the console, flipping switches and pulling levers as the engines roared to life. Yaz leaned against the railing, her chest heaving. "What was that thing?"

The Doctor didn't look up, his hands moving in a blur. "A remnant. A fragment of something ancient, drawn to the fear we banished. It's not the Boogeyman, but it's connected."

The TARDIS jolted, the lights flickering as the shadow battered against its defenses. Yaz steadied herself, her voice rising. "Can we escape it?"

The Doctor's eyes blazed with determination as he pulled the final lever. "Not just escape, Yaz. We're going to find out what it wants and stop it. Because no shadow gets to tell us when to run."

The TARDIS surged forward, leaving the collapsing dimension behind. But the Doctor knew this was just the beginning. The Boogeyman was gone, but fear had many faces, and one of them had just made its presence known.

Chapter 25: The Doctor's Next Adventure

The TARDIS hummed steadily as it drifted through the time vortex. Yaz sat cross-legged on the floor near the console, flipping through one of the Doctor's many scattered books—this one on the nature of paradoxes. She wasn't entirely sure if she was reading it for curiosity or distraction. The shadowy figure they'd just encountered lingered in the back of her mind, its voice echoing faintly.

The Doctor was unusually quiet, tinkering with the console while muttering under his breath. His movements were precise but lacked the manic energy Yaz had grown accustomed to.

"You alright, Doctor?" Yaz finally asked, closing the book and standing. "You've been unusually... calm."

The Doctor looked up, blinking as though just realizing she was there. "Calm? No, no, Yaz. Not calm. Thinking. Big difference."

"Thinking about what?" Yaz pressed, leaning against the console. "The shadow thing? Or the Boogeyman?"

The Doctor's lips twitched into a faint smile, but it didn't reach his eyes. "Both, actually. Fear has a way of leaving echoes, Yaz. Even when the source is gone, the ripples it creates can linger. Sometimes for centuries."

Yaz frowned. "Do you think it's over? I mean, the Boogeyman and his lot?"

The Doctor straightened, brushing his coat as he met her gaze. "For this town, yes. For now. But fear doesn't play fair—it's always looking for the next foothold. The trick is making sure the people it targets know how to fight back."

Before Yaz could reply, the TARDIS emitted a high-pitched beep. The console's lights flickered, and a small, holographic interface sprang to life. The Doctor's demeanor changed instantly, his previous introspection replaced with focused curiosity.

"Ah, what have we here?" he said, bounding to the console and adjusting the settings. The hologram sharpened into the image of a pale, wide-eyed woman, her expression panicked.

"Help… please, someone help us!" the woman cried, her voice crackling with static. Behind her, a chaotic scene unfolded—a metallic corridor lit by flickering red lights, with shadowy figures darting in the background.

"Distress call!" the Doctor exclaimed, a spark of excitement in his eyes. "And a good one, too. High stakes, lots of running, and potentially life-threatening danger. Just what we needed!"

Yaz sighed, already grabbing her jacket. "You're a bit too enthusiastic about the 'life-threatening danger' part, Doctor."

The Doctor spun around, grinning. "Oh, Yaz. It's not the danger—it's the challenge. New puzzles to solve, new people to save. What's not to love?"

The TARDIS shuddered as the Doctor input the coordinates, its engines roaring to life. Yaz steadied herself, her adrenaline kicking in as she prepared for whatever awaited them.

The TARDIS materialized with a heavy thunk, the interior lights dimming momentarily as the engines powered down. The Doctor grabbed his coat from the railing and strode to the doors, throwing them open with his usual flair.

They stepped into a stark, industrial corridor, the walls lined with exposed pipes and flickering lights. The air smelled of oil and something metallic, almost like blood. Alarms blared in the distance, accompanied by the faint sound of panicked voices.

Yaz wrinkled her nose. "Where are we?"

The Doctor examined the walls, his sonic screwdriver buzzing as he scanned. "Some sort of spaceship. Big one, by the looks of it. Cargo hauler? No, too sleek for that. Research vessel, perhaps?"

"Doctor!" Yaz pointed ahead, where a woman—the same one from the distress call—stumbled into view. She clutched her arm, blood seeping through her fingers.

"Help!" the woman gasped, collapsing to her knees.

The Doctor sprinted forward, kneeling beside her and pulling out a small medical kit from his coat. "Hello there! I'm the Doctor, and this is Yaz. What's your name?"

"L-Lyra," the woman stammered, wincing as the Doctor wrapped her arm in a bandage. "You... you got our signal?"

The Doctor nodded, his expression kind but focused. "We did. What's happening here, Lyra? What are we dealing with?"

Lyra's eyes darted around, her breath hitching. "The shadows... they came out of nowhere. They're taking people—dragging them into the dark. We tried to fight, but—"

The Doctor's face darkened, and he exchanged a quick glance with Yaz. "Shadows, you say? Did they look like living smoke? Red eyes?"

Lyra nodded frantically. "Yes! You've seen them?"

Yaz swallowed hard. "Yeah, we've seen them. Doctor, it's the same thing, isn't it? From the Boogey World."

The Doctor stood, his expression grave. "No. Not exactly. But it's connected. Whatever this is, it's spreading, adapting. And it's gotten clever."

Lyra clutched his arm, her voice desperate. "Can you stop it?"

The Doctor's eyes flashed with determination. "Of course I can. But first, I need to understand it. Yaz, stay with Lyra. I'm going to investigate."

Yaz grabbed his arm. "Oh no, you don't. You're not running off alone again."

The Doctor hesitated, then nodded. "Fair point. Come on, Yaz. Let's see what's lurking in the shadows."

As they moved deeper into the ship, the corridors grew darker, the flickering lights casting ominous shapes on the walls. The Doctor scanned constantly with his sonic screwdriver, his brow furrowed in concentration.

"It's not just attacking people," he muttered. "It's feeding. Drawing energy from their fear and using it to expand."

Yaz shivered. "Like the Boogeyman?"

"Similar, but more deliberate," the Doctor said. "The Boogeyman thrived on chaos. This... this feels calculated. Directed."

They turned a corner and froze. Ahead of them, a thick, black mass writhed on the floor, pulsing like a living heart. It stretched toward them, tendrils snaking along the walls and ceiling.

The Doctor stepped forward, his voice low and steady. "Hello there. I'm the Doctor. Care to tell me what you're doing on this lovely spaceship?"

The mass hissed, its tendrils retracting slightly. A deep, guttural voice echoed through the corridor. "Time Lord... always interfering. You cannot stop what is inevitable."

Yaz pulled out her flashlight, aiming the beam at the mass. It recoiled with a shriek, shrinking back into the shadows.

The Doctor grinned. "Ah, you don't like light, do you? That's your weakness."

The shadow mass shuddered, its voice venomous. "We are everywhere. We are eternal. You cannot escape the dark."

The Doctor's grin widened. "Maybe not. But I can shine a light bright enough to burn you away."

He turned to Yaz, his voice brisk. "Get back to the TARDIS. Activate the ship's photonic array—it's keyed to my sonic screwdriver. I'll hold this thing off."

Yaz hesitated, her flashlight trembling slightly. "Doctor—"

"Go, Yaz!" he barked, his eyes fierce. "This is just the beginning. And if we're going to win this fight, we need every advantage we can get."

Yaz nodded, her jaw tightening. "Be careful."

As she ran, the Doctor turned back to the writhing shadow, his sonic screwdriver buzzing to life. His voice echoed through the corridor, steady and fearless.

"You're not the first shadow I've faced, and you won't be the last. But you'll learn the same lesson they all did: the light always wins."

The shadow lunged, and the Doctor stood his ground, ready for the next battle in a fight that had only just begun.

Epilogue: Whispers in the Shadows

The TARDIS floated silently through the time vortex, its soothing hum a stark contrast to the tense atmosphere within. The Doctor leaned against the console, staring at the swirling patterns on the monitor. His usual exuberance was absent, replaced by a pensive silence that Yaz had come to recognize.

Yaz sat across from him, her arms crossed. "You've got that look again, Doctor."

The Doctor glanced at her, his expression unreadable. "What look?"

"The one that says you're thinking about something you don't want to talk about," Yaz replied, sitting up straighter. "What is it? The shadows?"

The Doctor hesitated, his hand brushing the edge of the console. "It's always the shadows, Yaz. They're everywhere. Every world, every time. They hide in corners, waiting for moments of doubt, weakness, fear. And no matter how many times we fight them, they always find a way back."

Yaz frowned. "But we stopped them. The Boogeyman, the shadows on that ship—they're gone."

The Doctor smiled faintly, but it didn't reach his eyes. "Gone? For now, maybe. But fear never truly disappears. It adapts, changes form. It's always there, waiting for the right moment to strike."

Far beyond the reach of the TARDIS, in a dimension sealed off by golden threads of light, the remnants of the Boogeyman stirred. The once-vivid landscapes of the Boogey World were now lifeless and barren, fading into a void of silence. But within the deepest shadows, a faint, rhythmic pulse echoed—a heartbeat that refused to fade.

The Boogeyman's fragmented form swirled in the darkness, his once-towering shape reduced to a shifting mass of shadows. His red eyes, though dimmed, still glowed faintly, burning with the embers of fury and hunger.

From the shadows, a voice emerged, fractured and layered. "You think you have won, Doctor. But fear is eternal."

The Boogeyman's gaze turned inward, focusing on the cracks in his prison. The golden seals that had banished him flickered faintly, holding firm but not impenetrable. He reached out with his essence, testing the edges of his confinement.

"Hope is a fleeting light," he hissed, his voice resonating in the void. "It burns brightly, but it fades. And when it does, I will return."

Back in the TARDIS, Yaz leaned against the console, her voice cutting through the Doctor's introspection. "You said fear always comes back. But so does hope, doesn't it? As long as people remember that, the shadows can't win."

The Doctor looked at her, his expression softening. "You're right, Yaz. Hope is the one thing fear can't fully extinguish. It's why I keep going. Why I do what I do. To remind people that even in the darkest moments, there's always a way out."

Yaz smiled. "So, what now? Another adventure?"

The Doctor straightened, his hands flying over the controls. "Oh, you know me, Yaz. The universe doesn't let me rest for long. Wherever there's darkness, there's someone who needs a bit of light."

The TARDIS groaned to life, its engines echoing through the console room. Yaz gripped the railing as the ship lurched forward, plunging them into the unknown.

Back in the Boogey World, the shadows stirred with renewed energy. The Boogeyman's voice echoed through the void, growing stronger with each passing moment.

"They will forget, in time. The Doctor will move on. And when the light dims... I will rise again."

His laughter reverberated through the empty dimension, a chilling reminder that fear was never truly defeated—it merely waited, lurking in the shadows, biding its time for the right moment to strike.

And in the vast expanse of the multiverse, where countless worlds teetered between hope and despair, the Boogeyman's whispers traveled like a cold wind, a faint but persistent promise that fear was eternal.

<u>Message from the Author:</u>

I hope you enjoyed this book, I love astrology and knew there was not a book such as this out on the shelf. I love metaphysical items as well. Please check out my other books:

-Life of Government Benefits

-My life of Hell

-My life with Hydrocephalus

-Red Sky

-World Domination:Woman's rule

-World Domination:Woman's Rule 2: The War

-Life and Banishment of Apophis: book 1

-The Kidney Friendly Diet

-The Ultimate Hemp Cookbook

-Creating a Dispensary(legally)

-Cleanliness throughout life: the importance of showering from childhood to adulthood.

-Strong Roots: The Risks of Overcoddling children

-Hemp Horoscopes: Cosmic Insights and Earthly Healing

- Celestial Hemp Navigating the Zodiac: Through the Green Cosmos

-Astrological Hemp: Aligning The Stars with Earth's Ancient Herb

-The Astrological Guide to Hemp: Stars, Signs, and Sacred Leaves

-Green Growth: Innovative Marketing Strategies for your Hemp Products and Dispensary

-Cosmic Cannabis

-Astrological Munchies

-Henry The Hemp

-Zodiacal Roots: The Astrological Soul Of Hemp

- **Green Constellations: Intersection of Hemp and Zodiac**

-Hemp in The Houses: An astrological Adventure Through The Cannabis Galaxy

-Galactic Ganja Guide

Heavenly Hemp

Zodiac Leaves

Doctor Who Astrology

Cannastrology

Stellar Satvias and Cosmic Indicas

<u>Celestial Cannabis: A Zodiac Journey</u>

AstroHerbology: The Sky and The Soil: Volume 1

AstroHerbology:Celestial Cannabis:Volume 2

Cosmic Cannabis Cultivation

The Starry Guide to Herbal Harmony: Volume 1

The Starry Guide to Herbal Harmony: Cannabis Universe: Volume
2

Yugioh Astrology: Astrological Guide to Deck, Duels and more

Nightmare Mansion: Echoes of The Abyss

Nightmare Mansion 2: Legacy of Shadows

Nightmare Mansion 3: Shadows of the Forgotten

Nightmare Mansion 4: Echoes of the Damned

The Life and Banishment of Apophis: Book 2

Nightmare Mansion: Halls of Despair

<u>Healing with Herb: Cannabis and Hydrocephalus</u>

<u>Planetary Pot: Aligning with Astrological Herbs: Volume 1</u>

Fast Track to Freedom: 30 Days to Financial Independence Using AI, Assets, and Agile Hustles

<u>Cosmic Hemp Pathways</u>

How to Become Financially Free in 30 Days: 10,000 Paths to Prosperity

Zodiacal Herbage: Astrological Insights: Volume 1

Nightmare Mansion: Whispers in the Walls

The Daleks Invade Atlantis

Henry the hemp and Hydrocephalus

10X The Kidney Friendly Diet

Cannabis Universe: Adult coloring book

Hemp Astrology: The Healing Power of the Stars

Zodiacal Herbage: Astrological Insights: Cannabis Universe: Volume 2

<u>Planetary Pot: Aligning with Astrological Herbs: Cannabis Universes: Volume 2</u>

Doctor Who Meets the Replicators and SG-1: The Ultimate Battle for Survival

Nightmare Mansion: Curse of the Blood Moon

<u>The Celestial Stoner: A Guide to the Zodiac</u>

Cosmic Pleasures: Sex Toy Astrology for Every Sign

Hydrocephalus Astrology: Navigating the Stars and Healing Waters

Lapis and the Mischievous Chocolate Bar

Celestial Positions: Sexual Astrology for Every Sign

Apophis's Shadow Work Journal: : A Journey of Self-Discovery and Healing

Kinky Cosmos: Sexual Kink Astrology for Every Sign

Digital Cosmos: The Astrological Digimon Compendium

Stellar Seeds: The Cosmic Guide to Growing with Astrology

Apophis's Daily Gratitude Journal

Cat Astrology: Feline Mysteries of the Cosmos

The Cosmic Kama Sutra: An Astrological Guide to Sexual Positions

Unleash Your Potential: A Guided Journal Powered by AI Insights

Whispers of the Enchanted Grove

Cosmic Pleasures: An Astrological Guide to Sexual Kinks

369, 12 Manifestation Journal

Whisper of the nocturne journal(blank journal for writing or drawing)

The Boogey Book

Locked In Reflection: A Chastity Journey Through Locktober

Generating Wealth Quickly:

How to Generate $100,000 in 24 Hours

Star Magic: Harness the Power of the Universe

The Flatulence Chronicles: A Fart Journal for Self-Discovery

The Doctor and The Death Moth

Seize the Day: A Personal Seizure Tracking Journal

The Ultimate Boogeyman Safari: A Journey into the Boogie World and Beyond

Whispers of Samhain: 1,000 Spells of Love, Luck, and Lunar Magic: Samhain Spell Book

Apophis's guides:

Witch's Spellbook Crafting Guide for Halloween

<u>Frost & Flame: The Enchanted Yule Grimoire of 1000 Winter Spells</u>

<u>The Ultimate Boogey Goo Guide & Spooky Activities for Halloween Fun</u>

Harmony of the Scales: A Libra's Spellcraft for Balance and Beauty

The Enchanted Advent: 36 Days of Christmas Wonders

Nightmare Mansion: The Labyrinth of Screams

Harvest of Enchantment: 1,000 Spells of Gratitude, Love, and Fortune for Thanksgiving

The Boogey Chronicles: A Journal of Nightly Encounters and Shadowy Secrets

The 12 Days of Financial Freedom: A Step-by-Step Christmas Countdown to Transform Your Finances

Sigil of the Eternal Spiral Blank Journal

A Christmas Feast: Timeless Recipes for Every Meal

Holiday Stress-Free Solutions: A Survival Guide to Thriving During the Festive Season

Yu-Gi-Oh! Holiday Gifting Mastery: The Ultimate Guide for Fans and Newcomers Alike

Holiday Harmony: A Hydrocephalus Survival Guide for the Festive Season

Celestial Craft: The Witch's Almanac for 2025 – A Cosmic Guide to Manifestations, Moons, and Mystical Events

Doctor Who: The Toymaker's Winter Wonderland

Tulsa King Unveiled: A Thrilling Guide to Stallone's Mafia Masterpiece

Pendulum Craft: A Complete Guide to Crafting and Using Personalized Divination Tools

Nightmare Mansion: Santa's Eternal Eve

Starlight Noel: A Cosmic Journey through Christmas Mysteries

The Dark Architect: Unlocking the Blueprint of Existence

Surviving the Embrace: The Ultimate Guide to Encounters with The Hugging Molly

The Enchanted Codex: Secrets of the Craft for Witches, Wiccans, and Pagans

Harvest of Gratitude: A Complete Thanksgiving Guide

Yuletide Essentials: A Complete Guide to an Authentic and Magical Christmas

Celestial Smokes: A Cosmic Guide to Cigars and Astrology

Living in Balance: A Comprehensive Survival Guide to Thriving with Diabetes Insipidus

Cosmic Symbiosis: The Venom Zodiac Chronicles

The Cursed Paw of Ambition

Cosmic Symbiosis: The Astrological Venom Journal

Celestial Wonders Unfold: A Stargazer's Guide to the Cosmos (2024-2029)

The Ultimate Black Friday Prepper's Guide: Mastering Shopping Strategies and Savings

Cosmic Sales: The Astrological Guide to Black Friday Shopping
Legends of the Corn Mother and Other Harvest Myths
Whispers of the Harvest: The Corn Mother's Journal
The Evergreen Spellbook
If you want solar for your home go here: https://www.harborso-lar.live/apophisenterprises/

Get Some Tarot cards: https://www.makeplayingcards.com/sell/apophis-occult-shop

Get some shirts: https://www.bonfire.com/store/apophis-shirt-emporium/

<u>**Instagrams:**</u>
@apophis_enterprises,
@apophisbookemporium,
@apophisscardshop
Twitter: @apophisenterpr1
 Tiktok:@apophisenterprise
Youtube: @sg1fan23477, @FiresideRetreatKingdom
Hive: @sg1fan23477
CheeLee: @SG1fan23477

Podcast: Apophis Chat Zone: https://open.spotify.com/show/5zXbrCLEV2xzCp8ybrfHsk?si=fb4d4fdbdce44dec

Newsletter: https://apophiss-newsletter-27c897.beehiiv.com/